"I Just Do[n't Want To] Change Us…Y[ou Know What I Mean?]"

He kissed her lips, gently, slowly. Kissed his way along her jawline, down the long, slender column of her throat, pleased when she tilted her head back and groaned. He'd dreamed of this moment for so long. Longer than he liked to admit, even to himself. He'd never allowed any woman to have such control over his mind or his fantasies.

"Nothing will change," he assured her between kisses. "Unless it's better. And I'm positive in the next few minutes, things between us will get a whole lot better."

Victoria's arms circled around his neck as her head turned, her mouth colliding with his.

And that's when the dam burst. His, hers. Did it matter? He'd wanted her for years and whether she'd wanted him that long or she'd just decided it in the past few weeks they'd been together, he didn't know, but he did know he was going to have her. Now. Here.

Dear Reader,

There is no way to express my love for this story on this one single page. As I was working on my Hollywood series, I watched the beautiful wedding of William and Kate. The little girl inside of me started daydreaming, and I just knew Victoria Dane deserved a fairy tale of her own.

Victoria captured my attention from the moment she was introduced in *Caught in the Spotlight*. But Prince Stefan… oh, he stole my heart before I ever typed Chapter One. With his love for his country, his loyalty to Victoria and all those tattoos (insert dreamy sigh) he is definitely a hero you won't soon forget.

Prince Stefan is a man who always thought he was in control of his wants, but it took him a while to come to grips with the fact he's in love with his best friend. And, believe me, there's nothing like falling in love with your best friend. I married mine. :)

What I love about Stefan and Victoria is they don't even try to fight their attraction. They dive in headfirst and worry about the consequences later...and that's when their troubles begin. But, these two are fighters and they will not back down—no matter what they have to give up in exchange for love.

The only drawback to this book is that it had to come to an end. I hope you enjoy Prince Stefan and Victoria's story as much as I did, and I hope you're living your own fairy tale.

Happy reading!

Jules

JULES BENNETT

BEHIND PALACE DOORS

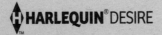

Recycling programs
for this product may
not exist in your area.

ISBN-13: 978-0-373-73232-6

BEHIND PALACE DOORS

Printed in U.S.A.

Books by Jules Bennett

Harlequin Desire

Her Innocence, His Conquest #2081
Caught in the Spotlight #2148
Whatever the Price #2181
Behind Palace Doors #2219

Silhouette Desire

Seducing the Enemy's Daughter #2004
For Business...or Marriage? #2010
From Boardroom to Wedding Bed? #2046

Other titles by this author available in ebook format.

JULES BENNETT

National bestselling author Jules Bennett's love of storytelling started when she would get in trouble as a child and would tell her parents her imaginary friends were to blame. Since then, her vivid imagination has taken her down a path she'd only dreamed of. And after twelve years of owning and working in salons, she hung up her shears to write full-time.

Jules doesn't just write Happily Ever After, she lives it. Married to her high school sweetheart, Jules and her hubby have two little girls who keep them smiling. She loves to hear from readers! Contact her at authorjules@gmail.com, visit her website, www.julesbennett.com, where you can sign up for her newsletter, or send her a letter at P.O. Box 396, Minford, OH 45653. You can also follow her on Twitter and join her Facebook fan page.

I'm dedicating this fairy tale to my stiletto-wearing, tiara-worthy glitter sister, Kelly Willison, and her beautiful princess in training, Anna. You two are a bright, shimmering light in my life. The glow may be all the glitter, but I think it comes from your heart of gold. Love you both.

And also to my own little princesses, Grace and Madelyn. I love watching you grow into beautiful little girls. I can't wait to see you fall in love and live your own fairy-tale dream.

Prologue

"Ever tried skinny-dipping?"

Victoria Dane gasped as Stefan Alexander, Prince of Galini Isle, stripped off his shirt.

"Umm…" She swallowed, watching as an impressive set of abs stared back at her. "No. No, I haven't."

He toed off his shoes.

"You're not going to…"

His soft chuckle caused goose bumps to spread over her body. Even at fifteen, she was totally aware of this handsome prince, who was technically a man, as he was three years older.

They'd quickly become friends since her mother was filming on his estate, and she assumed her girlish crush was normal. But was he really going to strip naked?

"I'm not doing it alone," he told her, hands on his hips.

Her eyes darted to his chest. "You got a tattoo?"

With a wicked grin, he nodded. "My first of many, I hope."

"What is it?" she asked, stepping closer to inspect.

Would it be rude to touch? Probably, so she slid her hands inside the pockets of her swim cover-up instead. Still, she imagined her fingertips sliding along the new ink.

"It's my family's crest," he told her. "I thought it appropriate to have that as my first. Besides, my father might not mind as much since it's symbolic."

The afternoon sun beat down on her, but Victoria knew the heat consuming her had nothing to do with the weather. She'd been on location with her mother for almost two months now, and she and Stefan had clicked from the moment they met. Of course, he probably saw her as a little sister and had no idea she was halfway in love with him.

The boys back home were nothing like this.

"Has your father seen it yet?" she asked, using the tattoo excuse to continue to stare at his chest.

"Nah. I've been careful to keep my shirt on around my dad since I got it two weeks ago. He'll throw a fit, but it's done, so what can he say now?"

Victoria moved toward the pool, dropped to the side and let her feet dangle in the cool water. "You're so relaxed about breaking rules and defying people. Aren't you worried you'll get in serious trouble one day?"

"Trouble?" He laughed as he sat down and joined her. "I'm not afraid of trouble. I'd rather be myself and live my life the way I want. I don't want to be ruled by what is considered to be the right thing. Who's to say what's right or wrong for me?"

She admired his take-charge attitude about life. He reminded her of her brother, Bronson.

"Don't you consider that lying?" she asked, still studying him. "I mean, you knew you were going to do it, so why not just tell your dad?"

Stefan glanced over to her, those bright blue eyes holding hers. "Lying by omission doesn't count in my book."

"Well, it does in mine. Maybe that's a cultural difference."

He scooped a hand in the water and playfully tossed it up onto her bare thighs. Shivers coursed through her.

"I think it's the difference between towing the line and living in the moment," he joked. "So how about that skinny-dipping?"

"I tow the line, remember? No skinny-dipping for me." Smiling at him, she placed a hand on his back and shoved him into the pool.

One

Every little girl envisioned a fairy-tale wedding. The long white train, the horse-drawn carriage, like the magical coach from Cinderella of course, and the proverbial tall, dark and handsome prince, chest adorned with medals and a bright blue sash that matched his eye color perfectly.

And while Victoria Dane wasn't living the fairy tale herself, she did have the glorious job of designing the royal wedding dress that would be seen by millions and worn by the next queen of Galini Isle.

Okay, so being the designer wasn't even a close second to becoming a queen.

"Victoria."

The familiar, soothing tone of her old friend's voice had Victoria turning from the breathtaking emerald ocean view. With a slight bow as was custom in this country, Victoria greeted the prince.

With his tight-fitting black T-shirt tucked into designer

jeans, most people would have a hard time believing Prince Stefan Alexander—owner of the most impressive set of blue eyes and some new ink peeking beneath the sleeve of his shirt on one impressive bicep—was the next in line to reign over this beautiful land.

Those muscles seemed to grow between each of their visits. Muscles he acquired from his passion of rock climbing. Yeah, that would make for a beautiful picture. A golden Greek god, shirtless and dangling high above the ground by his sheer strength....

There was one lucky bride waiting for her prince. Victoria would be lying if she didn't admit, even if only to herself, that at one time she'd envisioned herself as the one who would finally tame the great Prince Alexander, but his friendship had been invaluable and something she'd feared risking.

Strong arms that she had missed for the past few years pulled her into a warm, inviting embrace. Yes, this was the connection, the bond that phone calls and emails couldn't deliver.

"Prince Alexander," she said, returning his embrace.

"Don't 'Prince Alexander' me." His rich laughter enveloped her, making her feel even more excited to see him after so long. "And for God's sake, don't bow. Just because we haven't seen each other in a while doesn't mean I've become some royal snob."

"It's so great to see you, Stefan." She eased back and looked up into those striking blue eyes. "When you called to tell me you were getting married, I was shocked. She must be someone very special."

"The most important woman in my life," he said, lifting one of her hands to his lips.

Prince Charming had nothing on Stefan, and a slight surge of jealousy speared through Victoria at the fact another woman would be entering his life…and not just passing through like all the others.

He gestured toward the settee and matching chairs with bright orange plush cushions. "Let's have a seat and discuss my beautiful bride, shall we?"

Stefan dismissed his assistants with a silent nod. A man of his position and power didn't need to use words, but to Victoria he was still that rotten teen who'd tried to get her to go skinny-dipping in the royal pool…while a dinner party had been taking place in the grand ballroom.

"I've brought sketches of several dresses for you and your fiancée to review," she told him, laying her thin portfolio of designs on the tile tabletop and flipping it open. "I can also combine styles or come up with something completely different if nothing here catches her eye. They are all classic designs but different in their own way. Any would be flattering for the next queen."

"I've no doubt you'll make the perfect dress." He laid a hand over hers, a wide grin spreading across his devilishly handsome face. "It's so great to have you here, Victoria. I've missed you."

She returned his smile, unable to hide her excitement about not only seeing him again, but also the fact he'd finally found true love…something she'd started to have doubts about. And yes, she'd once wished his true love had been her, but their friendship was more important. As his best friend, she was thrilled that he was so happy and in love. She needed that reminder that not all men broke their promises of engagement.

"It's my pleasure to design for you, and it gives us both a reason to set aside our busy lives and get some face time," she told him, sliding her hair over her shoulder. "Phone calls just aren't the same."

"No, they're not," he agreed.

That sexy, sultry smile remained. Heavens, but the man was literally a tall, dark and handsome prince, and that cotton shirt stretched so perfectly over his broad shoulders and chiseled biceps. She wondered what the new tattoo was of, but if she knew Stefan, he'd find a reason to shed his shirt in no time.

Yeah, he'd changed over the years, and definitely in all the right places. Rock climbing does a body good.

"These are remarkable," he told her as he fingered through the drawings. "Did you do these yourself or do you have a team?"

A burst of pride ran through her. She may be one of the most sought-out designers, but each client earned her undivided attention and she loved hearing praise for her hard work…especially coming from such a good friend.

"I have a small team, but these are all my own. I was selfish when it came to your bride." She moved one thick sheet to the side, eager to display the rest of her designs. "I'm partial to this one. The clean lines, the cut of the neckline and the molding of the bodice. Classy, yet sexy."

Very similar to the one she'd designed for own wedding. Of course that had been six months, a slew of bad press and one shattered heartache ago when her up-and-coming actor/fiancé decided to publicly destroy Victoria. But working with Stefan and his fiancée would help her to remember that happily ever afters do exist.

When she'd met him as a teen on the set of one of her mother's films, she'd developed an instant crush. He'd been a very mature eighteen years old, compared to her fifteen, with golden skin and a smile she'd come to appreciate that held just a touch of cockiness.

She'd been smitten to say the least, but they'd soon developed a friendship that had lasted through the years. Fantasies had come and gone…and come again where she'd envisioned him proposing to her and professing his hidden, undying passion. But those were little girl dreams. Besides, Stefan always had a companion or two at all times.

"You would look beautiful in that gown."

Victoria shook off her crazy thoughts and jerked her attention to Stefan.

"Sorry. I realize your own engagement is still fairly recent, but—"

She straightened her shoulders and stepped back. "No, it's okay. But let's not talk about that. I'd much rather focus on your happiness."

He reached out, cupped her shoulders and gave a reassuring squeeze. "I'm still your friend. I know you didn't open up that much over the phone because of the timing being so close to the passing of my father, but you're here now and I'm offering you my shoulder if you need it."

Warmth spread through her. Other than her brothers, this was the one man she'd always been able to depend on. Even as they'd gotten older, their lives busier, she knew Stefan was always there for her.

"I may take you up on that," she told him with a smile. "But for now let's discuss you."

Because she needed to focus on their friendship and her work instead of her humiliation, her eyes drifted back over the designs. "A dress should make a woman feel beautiful and alluring. I wanted to capture that beauty with a hint of fairy tale thrown into the mix. When I don't know the client personally, it makes designing the dresses a bit harder, so that is why I chose to bring very different designs for her to look at. Do you know when your fiancée will arrive?"

Stefan leaned a hip onto the table and smiled. "Actually, she's already here. I have a proposition for you, Victoria."

Intrigued, Victoria rested one hand on the table and smiled. "And what is that, Your Highness?"

He chuckled. "Now you're mocking me."

"Not at all," she retorted with a grin, loving how they fell back into their easy banter as if no time had passed. "You just sounded so serious. What's your proposition?"

He took her hands in his, looking her in the eyes. "It has to do with my fiancée…sort of."

Oh, no. She recognized that look. It was the same naughty, conniving look he had when he'd wanted her to be his partner in crime in their early twenties…like the time when he'd asked her to pose as his girlfriend for a charity ball because he had a somewhat aggressive lady who wouldn't take no for an answer.

God. The sick feeling in her stomach deepened. The man was up to something no good.

"Stefan." She slid her hands from his warm, strong hold and rubbed them together. "Tell me there's a real fiancée and you're actually getting married."

"I am getting married and there is a fiancée." He threw her a wide, beautiful smile. "You."

Stefan waited for her response to his abrupt proposal. Damn, he'd meant to have a bit more finesse, but time was running out and he couldn't afford to tackle this wedding in the traditional sense. Nothing about this situation was traditional.

She placed her hands on either side of her temples as if to rub the stress headache away…he'd had a few of those moments himself recently. He'd never pictured himself as a one-woman man. And the thought always sent a shudder straight through him.

"I'm sorry to pull you into this," he told her. "I couldn't trust anyone else right now."

He prayed he chose the right words to make her understand. She was, after all, still recovering from an ugly public breakup, and she had always been such a good friend, no matter the distance between them. They'd shared countless phone calls in the middle of the night, during many of which she'd told him her dreams and he'd listened, hoping one day all those dreams would come true. And perhaps he could help that along.

"Why do you need me all of a sudden?"

"Galini Isle will go back to Greece if I don't marry and gain the title of king. My brother isn't an option because his wife is a divorcée and the damn laws are archaic. I couldn't live with myself if I didn't do everything in my power to keep this country in my family. I won't let my people down." He hated being forced into anything. "I want my title, but I do not want a wife. Unfortunately, I've looked for a loophole and there isn't one."

Victoria sank to the patio chair. "Again, why me?"

"I want a wife in name only. And I can't let my country revert to Greek rule. It's been in my family for generations. I refuse to be a failure to my family's name."

"This is crazy," she muttered, shaking her head.

Stefan stepped closer. "You've recently had scandal in your life. Why not show this fiancé who jilted you and the media who exploited your pain that you are stronger, you can rise above this and come out on top? What better way than to marry a prince?"

"You're serious?" she asked, looking back up at him. "How could we pull this off? I mean, we haven't been seen together in public for a couple years."

Stefan came over and took a seat directly beside her in the matching wrought-iron chair with plush cushions. "My people don't know who my bride is. I've made sure they only know there will be a wedding. I've been very secretive about this, which only adds to the mystery of the romance."

Romance. Yeah, that was the dead last thing on his mind right now. Couldn't he just have the crown? He was the prince, for crying out loud. Didn't that give him some clout? Why did he need a marriage to claim it?

"Once they see you, they'll know why I kept the engagement so quiet," he went on, knowing he was rambling, but he had to make her see this was the only way.

Damn, he hated vulnerability and being backed into a corner. Not only that, he hated putting Victoria in an awkward position.

Victoria laughed. "And here all this time I thought you were letting your romantic, protective side show."

"You are one of Hollywood's most famous single ladies—a bachelorette, I believe your country calls it—and I will simply explain I was protecting you from even more scandal and we wanted to express our love on our wedding day and not exploit it beforehand. Besides, there are all those articles and pictures from when we were in our teens and twenties. The media practically had us engaged at your twenty-first birthday party when I bought you a diamond necklace. The history is there, and the media will eat it up."

"Oh, Stefan." She sighed. "This is such a big decision. You can't expect me to give you an answer right now."

Leaning back against the chair, Stefan nodded. "I'm asking for only six months, Tori. After my coronation I'll have my title as king and the country will be secured with my family again."

"Then what?" she asked, her eyes searching his.

He shrugged, not really worried about anything beyond getting married and gaining his title. "After that it's up to you. You can stay married to me or you can end the relationship. The control is yours. Who knows, you may like being queen."

True, he may be a playboy, but he could think of multiple circumstances that would be worse than being married to the stunning Victoria Dane.

She stared out across the estate toward the ocean. Victoria's beauty was remarkable and surprisingly natural. She came from the land of perfection brought on by plastic surgeons, yet she looked more stunning than the fake, siliconed women he knew. And he was damn lucky she was in his life.

"This is the craziest thing I've ever heard." With a slight laugh she looked back to him. "You're taking something as serious as a royal wedding, a wedding that will create the new leaders for your country, and turning it into a…a lie. My God, Stefan, this is really putting the pressure on our friendship. Do you realize how risky this is? I can't lose you."

He sat forward, dead serious. "You could never lose me as a friend. If I thought that was the case I never would've asked you. Just think of this as a long, overdue reunion. I need someone I can trust not to back out at the last minute or use me for money in the end."

"Why did you wait so long to ask me?"

"Honestly I thought I could find a way around this." God knows he'd exhausted every avenue looking for one. "When I realized I couldn't, I knew I had only one option. You are the one person in my life I'd ever trust with something so personal, so serious."

She laughed. "I'd do anything for you, Stefan, you know that, but this is asking a lot. What about the people of your country? Won't they feel let down if we end the marriage? And how will this work out after your coronation? Will the country still remain yours?"

"No, my people won't feel let down," he assured her. "I will still be their leader. I will still keep control over my country. I just need the title to do so, which is where you fit in."

"You've really thought this through, haven't you?" She crossed her legs and shifted her body toward his. "You can't expect me to put my life on hold for six months. I'm a busy woman, Stefan."

He'd always admired her take-charge attitude and the way she matched him in this volley of wills. Not to mention the fact the woman was classy and beyond sexy.

Just as when he'd been in his late teens, Victoria Dane made his gut clench and still made him want her as more than a friend. But years ago he'd attempted to pursue her into something sexual. She hadn't taken him seriously, so to keep his ego intact, he played it off like he had indeed been joking. And the second time he'd been ready to take charge, she'd been in a relationship. But now she was free.

"I know you're busy, and I'm not trying to take your life away, but I do have something to offer you." He edged forward, taking her hand in his. "You'll get to show the world that you are stronger than the poor, humiliated woman they are making you out to be. The woman the media has portrayed as being overshadowed by her brothers and jilted by her fiancé. If you do this, not only will you design your wedding gown for this day, this could help you launch that bridal line you've been wanting. Make a play off the fairy tale of being a queen, if you like."

Her eyes darted back to the ocean. The sun was just starting to set, and Stefan knew as far as proposals went, this was probably the least romantic. But her apparent inner war with herself only told him that she was indeed considering his offer.

"I can practically see your mind working." He hoped she was leaning toward a yes decision. "This is a win-win for both of us, Victoria."

"Your way of thinking is not very Greek," she told him. "Aren't you all known for love?"

He laughed, squeezing her hand. "I think you know how passionate I can be about something I want."

She looked down at their joined hands. His dark, tanned skin next to her pinker complexion made for quite the contrast. But when she looked up into his eyes, he knew she wasn't going to deny him.

"You've always been determined," she whispered. "That's something I can understand. With my recent scandal and public embarrassment, I was adamant to get back on track, to take control of my life."

He waited, not wanting to interrupt as she guided her own words down the path toward everything he wanted.

"And what about the sleeping arrangements?" she asked, her wide eyes seeking his for answers.

Stefan laughed. "You know, you live in Hollywood where sin flows as freely as wine in my country, and you're blushing at the subject of us sharing a bed. I'm wounded."

Obviously this was something she hadn't expected, but he wasn't going to push. Yes, he'd desired her for years, but he wanted her to come to him. To realize that maybe something spectacular could happen between them behind the bedroom door.

He stroked his thumb over the soft skin on the back of her hand. "We'll have to share a room to keep up the pretense with the staff."

Her heart beat hard against her chest, and Victoria couldn't help the image that immediately popped into her head of the two of them entangled in satin sheets in a king-size bed. She knew that his dark skin was part of his heritage and not from lounging by the pool—which meant he would be lean and golden brown all over. There were rumors of hidden tattoos—some she'd seen, some she hadn't. The man simply exuded mysteriousness and sex. He'd been her best friend as a teen, and even though circumstances had gotten in the way of them seeing each other the past couple years, their phone calls and emails had kept that line of friendship open.

"I just don't know," she muttered aloud. "I'm scared of what this will do to us."

"We'll be stronger than ever," he assured her with a devastatingly handsome smile. "We've spent too many of the past years apart. Let's just focus on the fact we'll be together like old times. I need you, Tori."

Was she really about to risk more scandal and the bond she shared with Stefan? Yes, because he meant that much to her, and if the tables were turned, she knew he'd drop everything to help her. Besides, she was a member of the prestigious Hollywood Danes; it wasn't as if scandal hadn't been part of her life before.

For years she'd been in the spotlight as the sister of Hollywood's hottest producer and daughter of the Grand Dane—her mother's Hollywood-dubbed nickname. The threat of scandal followed her family everywhere.

Stefan's family had also had their share of scandal surrounding his mother's death years ago. His loyalty to his family—and his country—to maintain control of the crown was everything to him. And she completely understood family loyalty.

As she thought about it, Victoria was liking Stefan's proposal more and more. How could she not consider showing the world she could still come out on top—and with a sexy Greek prince, at that?

When Alex had put a ring on her finger, she'd been so determined to have a lasting, loving marriage like her mother, her brothers. Victoria didn't want pity, didn't want people looking at her as though she may fall apart if they brought up the broken engagement. Unfortunately, that's exactly what her family and friends were doing. But Stefan faced the topic head-on and didn't back down. He wasn't treating her like some wilted flower, but as a woman who was tougher than what most people thought.

Victoria was determined to come out stronger on the other side of this scandal. She was going to prove to everyone, including herself, that her iconic mother and hot-shot brothers were not the only ones who could rise above anything life threw at them.

She looked down at her hand joined with Stefan's, knowing they could help each other…just like always. The arrangement was just on a larger scale than anything they'd ever confronted.

This proposition Stefan blindsided her with may truly be the answer to get everyone to stop throwing sympathy her way, to see that she was fine and had made her life her own. Not to mention she could use the publicity to help establish her bridal line, as he'd suggested. What better way to launch it than to design the royal wedding dress *and* wear it?

"You're thinking too hard," Stefan joked. "Go with your gut, Victoria. You know this is going to work. I won't let anything happen to you."

She looked into his vibrant eyes, confident he would do anything to keep her from facing heartache again. And that made his proposal even more appealing.

There was no denying the man was beyond sexy. He'd been dubbed the Greek Playboy Prince by all the media outlets for years. But Alex had been just as handsome, just as cocky…until he'd confessed he'd been using her for her family name to help further his acting career. Of course the truth had only come out after he'd impregnated another woman and had to call off the engagement.

Oh, how could she even sit here and compare the two men? Alex wasn't even worth her thoughts, and Stefan was everything to her.

Another look into his smiling eyes and Victoria nearly laughed. Stefan had been up-front and honest with her because that's the type of friend he was. What he was proposing was nothing like what Alex had done to her. Other than this marriage, what could she offer Stefan that he couldn't get himself? He certainly wasn't a rising actor like Alex had been. How could she deny him when she knew he was in a vulnerable state and he trusted only her?

"I'd expect you to be faithful, even if this is pretend," she told him.

"I assure you, you will have my undivided attention."

Swallowing the doubts and throwing caution to the wind, Victoria smiled. "Stefan, I'd be honored to marry you."

Two

Stefan had invited Victoria to stay in the palace so they could get some alone time to reconnect in ways that phone calls and emails couldn't provide. They had to attempt to make this seem like the real thing because the media would definitely pick up on any uncomfortableness between them if every touch, every lingering gaze didn't look authentic— like they were secret lovers.

Pretending to be infatuated by Victoria's beauty would be no hardship. Her flawless elegance had only flourished since the last time he'd seen her, and he was damned grateful she'd agreed to his insane proposal.

Parading her around the grounds with the royal photographer, snapping some pictures as they rode on horseback, cuddled beneath the trellis of flowing flowers and walked along the private, pristine beach, would help fuel this fire of his romance with the next queen of Galini Isle. Though he'd asked the photographer to keep Victoria's face out of the snapshots to add an aura of mystery. He'd always been proud and ready to show off the women on his arm. Victoria was the first one he'd protected from the camera. So once the photos started going out, they would hopefully create more talk of his upcoming wedding in four weeks.

Their brief time alone had already caused so many memories to resurface. She was still a tender heart where her family was concerned but lethal when it came to business. The beauty Victoria brought back into his life by being there in person was immeasurable. Holding her, laughing with her, staying up late last night talking again was amazing, and he vowed to never let so much time go between their visits again…if she ended up leaving at the end of the six months.

All thoughts of reconnecting were swept aside as Victoria entered the intimate dining area he'd had his assistants set up on the balcony off his master suite's second story. Stefan's breath caught, and he knew that spark of desire he'd always had for her would only spread and burn hotter now that they were spending so much intimate time alone.

Yes, he needed her to keep his country, but he wasn't a fool. No way would he let this prime opportunity pass him by to show her just how much he believed becoming friends with benefits was a great idea. He may not be ready for a "real" marriage, but he was past ready to have Victoria see him in a different way.

But he had to keep his thoughts and emotions to himself for now. The last thing she needed was him pushing anything more on her. Besides the fact she was saving him, she was coming out of a humiliating engagement to some prick who didn't know what a treasure he'd had.

When Stefan had initially learned of the breakup, he'd

immediately called, but in typical Victoria fashion, she'd assured him she was fine…hurt and angry, but she'd be okay.

And looking at her now, she was definitely more than okay.

Her long, strapless ice-blue chiffon gown was simple, yet so elegant and so beautifully molded to her slender curves, Stefan's palms itched to touch her. Years of friendship prevented him. Added to that, they'd never ventured into anything intimate. Either she'd been in a relationship or he'd been…preoccupied himself.

"You look beautiful, Victoria." He extended his hand toward her, pleased when she took it. "You'll be the perfect queen."

Her smile was genuine, but her eyes instantly darted to the waiting servant in the corner wearing a black tux. "I was hoping to have some time alone with you."

While he loved those words coming from her mouth, he knew she just wanted to talk. He squeezed her hand and gave a nod to his employee. Once they were alone, Victoria laughed.

"That's the second time you've nodded and someone has done what you wanted. You sure this prince-soon-to-be-king title isn't going to your head?"

Stefan shrugged, leading her to the table for two on the balcony. "They know what my needs are, so words are usually unnecessary. Besides, I'd much rather spend my evening with my stunning friend than boring staff. I have too many responsibilities with my title. I want to have the down time with you."

"Wow, I'm one rank above boring and responsibilities. You're such a charmer, it's no wonder you couldn't get another woman to marry you." She patted his arm and sighed. "I just hope my family understands my actions."

"We can't tell anyone that this is a paper marriage, Victoria." He turned her to face him, making her look him in the eye to know just how serious this situation was. "I cannot risk my title on the slip of a tongue."

He knew the strong bond she had with her family, knew she'd want to tell them, but he had to at least caution her as to the importance of this arrangement. Other than his personal assistant, Hector, and his brother, no one knew of this secret.

"I have to tell my mother," she insisted. "Trust me. She will know something is up and she will badger us both until she uncovers it if we don't confess now. Besides, she's always loved you."

"As a friend, yes," he agreed, then laughed. "I'm not sure she'll love me to play the son-in-law role."

She looked into his eyes, and a tilt of her perfect lips proved she knew he had a point. "Well, she does consider you a playboy, and she's not too keen on all your tats. But she does love you, Stefan. And she knows how much you mean to me."

He raised a brow. "What about your brothers?"

"I can't lie to them, either," she told him. "But you should know, of all families, mine understands the potential for scandal when secrets slip."

Because he could see the battle she waged with herself and because he knew she wouldn't back down on this, Stefan nodded. "If you promise this goes no further than your immediate family, I will agree to your terms. I trust them as much as I trust you."

"All right, Stefan," she told him, seeing his shoulders relax on his exhale. "My mother will be the silent observer until she sees if I'm just making a rash decision. But, I should warn you, my brothers will have some serious doubts. They will be all over you, especially after what happened with Alex."

Stefan intended to speak with both of her brothers privately. He had a business proposition for them that they may not want to pass up regarding a documentary to clear his parents' names in his mother's untimely death. Some thought his mother had committed suicide, while others were convinced his father had hired someone to have her killed. Both were pure nonsense, and he wanted to go into his reign with no blemishes on his family's name. But he would also reassure Tori's brothers that he would keep her from any more heartbreak or scandal.

"If I had a sister, I'd be very protective," he said with a smile. "I assure you, I can handle them. But we still have to make sure they know our relationship will have to look real, which means they'll have to rein in their behavior when we're out in the spotlight."

Stefan stepped closer, calling himself all kinds of a fool for torturing himself with her familiar floral aroma, her tall, lithe body close to his. But he couldn't help himself. He needed that intimacy, that closeness only Tori could provide. He told himself it was to get used to making this "relationship" seem real. In truth, he wanted to touch her, kiss her…undress her. Possibilities and images swirled around in his mind. Years he'd waited to have a chance with her, and here he was nervous as a virgin on a wedding night.

Na pari i eychi. Dammit. The last time he'd seen her in person two years ago he'd flown to L.A. to attend a benefit art show to raise money for a children's charity. His father was supposed to have gone but had fallen ill at the last minute, so Stefan had stepped in, all too eager to get to L.A. and try his hand at seducing Victoria.

But when he'd arrived at her home, she'd introduced him to some up-and-coming actor whom she'd just begun dating. Stefan had been totally blindsided with the sudden serious nature of the relationship. They talked on the phone, emailed or texted several times a week and no mention had been made of this other man.

Because she'd been beaming with happiness, Stefan had kept his lustful feelings to himself and tried to maintain a physical distance. But now she was here because that jerk, Alex, had humiliated her and crushed her heart.

Stefan had every intention of helping her heal. And now he knew there was no way he could hold his desire back. Eventually, he'd have to confess that he wanted her intimately, paper marriage be damned.

As if just realizing how close they'd gotten, Victoria looked up at him and licked her lips, making them moist and inviting. "I still think we have our work cut out for us. We've never been anything more than best friends."

It was just the opening he'd been waiting for. "Then we better start now making this believable."

In one move, Stefan had his arms snaked around her waist and his lips crushing hers, swallowing her gasp. He hadn't meant to push, really he hadn't, and the second their tastes and bodies collided, he knew this was a bad idea. Now he'd only want her more. But if his life depended on it, he couldn't pull away.

After the briefest of hesitations, she exploded in his arms, kissing him back with a passion he hadn't expected, but he would definitely embrace. For years he'd wondered, dreamed, and here she was kissing him as if she thought of him as a man and not just a friend. Obviously he wasn't the only one who'd imagined this moment.

And that aroused him even more and left him with the knowledge this was something that would have to be discussed sooner rather than later.

Needing more and taking it, he parted her lips with his tongue. Her fingers gripped his biceps as she leaned against him a bit more. And just like he'd imagined for years, she fit against him perfectly.

But before he could take more and allow his hands to roam freely over that killer body, Victoria stepped back, her hand immediately going to cover her lips.

"We can't…that was…"

Stefan closed the gap she'd just created, but not to pick up where she broke off. He intended to reassure her that what just happened was not a mistake. Hell no, it wasn't. An epiphany, yes, but no mistake.

"Interesting how flustered you are after one kiss," he told her with a smile, still tasting her on his lips. "We've kissed before, Tori."

With fingertips still on her lips, Victoria placed her other hand on his chest. "Our kisses were never anything like that."

Because he was a gentleman, at least where the ladies were concerned, he didn't mention the groaning she'd done when his lips had touched hers.

He wanted her to think about what happened… God knows he'd never forget. Her taste and the feel of her body were all burned into his long-term memory. But he needed to move slowly and stay on track.

"My top chef has prepared moussaka for us." He ushered her toward a chair and assisted her into it. "I remember how much you enjoyed Greek cuisine the last time you visited."

Victoria didn't even look at the meal; she merely gazed at him from across the intimate table complete with a small exotic bouquet of flowers and two tall white tapered candles.

"Are you going to pretend that kiss didn't make an impression on you?" she asked, arching a perfectly shaped brow.

Her bold statement had him smiling. Why lie? She knew him too well.

"I wasn't unaffected, Victoria." He held her gaze, needing her to see how serious he was. "Any man would be a fool not to be physically attracted to you. And I'd be a liar to say I hadn't thought of kissing you before."

"I'm not quite sure how to respond to that." She glanced down, then cleared her throat and met his gaze again. "I have to say, it's no wonder you have the reputation you do when you kiss like that. If you pull that stunt in public, the media will never think to question the engagement."

"They'll see nothing but *eros* when they look at us."

"What does that mean?" She laughed. "You always show off by throwing out Greek terms I don't know."

"Passionate, erotic love." Yet again, he held her gaze. "Cameras don't lie, and I know that's what they'll see. I will have no problem making the relationship look real."

Victoria shook her head. "I'm afraid your cockiness and ego may overshadow me in any picture, but I've found that ego charming over the years—must be from growing up with a very alpha brother. Your pride stems from confidence, which is always a redeeming quality in a man. But I know there's a soft side beneath that tough-guy persona. Besides, I've been around onlookers and cameras since I was born, so I actually don't notice them much anymore."

But they notice you.

"I'm glad to hear the media doesn't bother you because we'll have to pose for several formal pictures once we're married," he told her, taking the silver dome lids off the dishes. "Though something you may not be as used to is servants. As queen, you'll have your own assistants who will do anything and everything—from dressing you, to preparing your meals and escorting you anywhere you need to go."

Victoria's perfectly manicured hand stilled on her wine-glass. "I don't need someone to dress me—that's literally my job. And an escort? Is that really necessary? I can't stay here after the marriage until the title is official, Stefan. I have a life, a job to get to. If we need to put up a united front, you'll just have to come to the States and be with me there."

"For how long?" he asked. "With no one reigning as king, I am technically the…stand-in, if you will."

Victoria jerked in surprise. "You're acting as king now? I didn't know this."

He nodded. "Nothing is official until the coronation, but it's law that when the king dies, the oldest son will step in immediately. If something were to happen to me or if I did not marry, the country would go back to Greece. So this is all temporary until I fulfill my duties."

"So do you have to stay here the entire time?" she asked. "Are we going to spend our marriage apart?"

Stefan laughed. "Not at all. We will actually need to make several appearances together both here and in L.A. once we're married to ensure the public believes this is the real deal. What's your schedule like? We will come up with something."

His cell rang, interrupting their conversation. He pulled it from his pocket, glanced at the screen and hit ignore before sliding it back in his pocket…but not before Victoria saw the name of the caller. Hannah.

"Am I going to have to compete for your attention from your harem?" she asked with a laugh, even though inside she was dead serious.

"You will never have to compete for my attention, Tori." His eyes locked on to hers. "You're the only woman in my life right now. Let's get back to your schedule."

She wanted to believe him, so she did. He'd never lied

to her before, and she knew if Stefan told her not to worry, then she shouldn't. But no matter what his actions were, he couldn't force the other women to stop calling him. Surely once they were married the calls would stop. She hoped.

God, she was so skeptical. Damn Alex for making her that way. To doubt Stefan and his loyalty was laughable. He was going to great lengths to keep his country in his family. That act itself spoke volumes of what the word loyalty meant. So, no, she didn't think Stefan would do anything to betray her trust. He was the polar opposite of Alex.

"My workload is crazy." She ran her upcoming schedule through her head. "I'm swamped, but to be fair I'd say we should at least split the time between my home and yours."

"That shouldn't be a problem. I love your family and I love L.A." He moved around the table, unrolled her napkin and placed it in her lap, waiting until her eyes sought his. "But the first two weeks of our marriage, we are to remain in the palace. It's a tradition since the first king of Galini Isle. The country refers to it as the honeymoon phase."

Those expressive blue eyes widened. "I thought a honeymoon was when the couple went off to some undisclosed location to have privacy."

He tried to block the image of having her all to himself for two weeks. The instant erotic thoughts had him shifting back to his seat before he did something really embarrassing.

"This country prides itself on rituals. The *ethos,* or practice, is not to be dismissed."

Victoria stared at him from across the table. He could tell she was getting nervous, so he wanted to take her mind off what was to come.

"Tell me about what you're working on now, other than your own wedding dress," he added with a smile he knew would put her at ease.

In an instant her face softened, the corners of her mouth tilted up into a genuine smile and, yeah, he felt that straight to the gut. How would she look smiling up at him, hair spread across his pillow as he slid into her?

Damn. Now more than ever, he wanted her in his bed.

But he wouldn't pressure her. He'd wait until she was ready to come to him. And he had a feeling from that scorching kiss she'd be more than willing sooner rather than later.

Victoria was different than most women he dated, bedded. She was genuine. Rare in this world to find a woman this sexy and beautiful who didn't flaunt her body or use it to work her way through her goals. He'd always admired how she created a name for herself without riding on the coattails of her iconic family name.

"My brothers are working together on a film depicting our mother's life through the years. And I have to say they've gotten along so well since they put their differences aside and focused on our mother and this movie." She laughed, tossing her golden hair over one shoulder. "They're getting along so well, they even spend off hours together with their families. The kids at least provide a buffer and something else they have in common."

Stefan still couldn't wrap his mind around the fact Victoria's mother, the Grand Dane of Hollywood, gave up a child for adoption nearly forty years ago and the baby turned out to be Anthony Price, the long-time heated rival of Victoria's legitimate brother, Bronson Dane. Talk about confusing.

"I'm sure discovering Anthony was your half brother was quite a shock. I apologize for not being there more for you, but with my dad battling cancer then…"

"You were needed more here, Stefan." Victoria sipped her wine then picked up her fork. "I admit I was shocked, but my brothers took it the hardest. Mom gave Anthony up for adoption when she was starting in her career because she wanted him to have a good life and she wasn't ready for motherhood."

"That's a mature decision."

Victoria's eyes darted to his, and that sweet smile widened. "I knew you'd understand. You were always so open-minded. So many have called her decision selfish."

He shook his head, reaching for his own wineglass. "Selfish would've been keeping the baby, knowing she would put her career first."

She looked as if she wanted to say more, but she cut a piece of her meat and slid the fork between her perfectly painted pale pink lips. And like any man infatuated with a woman—or any man who had breath in his lungs—he agonizingly watched until the fork disappeared and she groaned with delight as her eyelids fluttered. Just when he thought his arousal couldn't get any stronger...

"This is still so amazing," she told him. "You have no idea how grateful I am that you remembered my favorite food."

He knew every single detail about her—her favorite color, the movies she'd seen countless times and even the old diary she kept all of her private thoughts in. He knew more about her than any other woman, which was why they had such a strong bond. He didn't mind listening to her talk about her life. Most other women talked about their lives in an attempt to impress him. Victoria impressed him simply by being there for him, making him smile and expecting nothing from him in return.

"So tell me about this film." He wanted to know more, wanted to support her. "What's your part?"

He also wanted to keep her relaxed, keep her talking all night—since that was his only option for now. Just like during their multiple phone conversations over the years, that sultry voice washed over him, making him wish for things he couldn't have right now. But at the end of this, who knew? Maybe they'd remain married. That would put quite a spin on the whole friends-with-benefits scenario.

He'd never had this type of arrangement before—even that would've been more of a commitment than he'd been willing to give. But for Victoria…hell yes, he'd be interested.

"I've never worked with my family before and never designed costumes for a movie, but I made an exception," she said with a glowing smile. "There's no way I could let another designer do this, not when it's so close to my heart."

"Sounds like you're going to be a busy woman," he told her, cutting into his tender meat.

"The designs are done since filming started a few months ago. But I'm needed on set in case of a malfunction or a last-minute wardrobe switch." She shrugged and sipped her wine. "My team back in L.A. is handling everything right now. My assistant may have to take on a bit more until our wedding is over, though. God, that sounds so strange to say."

He lay his fork down, reached across the table and took her hand. "Thank you for what you're doing for me, for my country. I'll never be able to express my gratitude."

"You've been my best friend since I had braces," she joked. "We may live far apart, but other than my family, you're the closest person in my life." She tightened her grip on his hand and tilted her head with a soft grin. "Besides, you've handed me a dream job designing the gown, and I get to play queen for a few months. Seriously, I'm getting the better end of the bargain."

Stefan laughed. "I wasn't sure you'd agree so easily. I should've known you'd stand by me."

"I admit I have reservations about lying to the public,

to my friends and employees." She shifted in her seat, breaking hold of their hands. "But I'm honored to stand by you. It's not often we find someone in our life we can truly depend on."

He hated the loss of her hands in his and the hurt in her tone. "I was afraid you'd be vulnerable since the breakup, afraid you'd shut this idea down before I could explain my reasons."

"Maybe I am still vulnerable." She chewed her lip, eyes darting down before coming back up to meet his. "But I won't let my heart get in the way of my life again, and I know I'm safe with you."

"Absolutely, Victoria." He'd die before he let her get hurt. "You know how much I care for you."

He admired Victoria for standing tall, not cowering behind her family when it would be so easy to do so after having her world ripped out from under her. He knew firsthand how hard life was to live in the public eye. The media was ruthless, and if the story wasn't there, they made one up and damn the consequences. Reputations could be damaged and ruined with just a small dose of ink from the written word and could take years to restore…if restoration was even possible.

Because of accusations thrown at his family after the death of his mother, he more than anyone knew how fast a reputation could be ruined.

The rest of the meal moved quickly through some laughter and easy conversation, but Stefan couldn't get his mind off that scorching kiss. He wanted his hands on her again, whether to torture himself or just have a brief moment of instant gratification, he didn't know. But he knew how to rectify the situation.

"Dance with me," he told her when she'd placed her napkin beside her now-empty plate.

"Right now?" She glanced around the spacious, moon-lit balcony. "There's no music."

He came to his feet, moved into the master suite and within seconds had the surround sound filtering out into the night. When he came back through the open double doors, he extended his hand.

"Dance with me," he repeated, pleased when her hand slid into his. "We should practice before the official royal wedding dance after the ceremony. It's been years since we danced together."

She came to her feet, and he took no time in pulling her body against his. Wrapping his arm around her waist, Stefan was more than eager to have her invade his personal space.

"No wonder you're the Playboy Prince," she murmured, her breath tickling his cheek. "You're very good at this. I can't imagine how you'd be pouring on the charm if I weren't an old childhood friend."

He eased his head back but kept their bodies flush and swaying to the soft, soothing beat. "I promised to keep this simple, to give you all control in the end. I never go against my word."

She smiled. "I'm sure you wouldn't, but I also know your reputation. And I was on the receiving end of that kiss."

"You weren't just on the receiving end…you were an active participant."

Victoria's breath caught. "That's a…pretty accurate statement, but we've been friends too long for us to let lust cloud our judgment. Sleeping together would not be wise, Stefan."

He leaned in close to her ear and whispered, "Who says?"

Her hand tightened in his as she turned to look him in the eye, their lips barely a breath apart. "I don't know if we're getting swept up into this idea of pretending or this physical pull is stemming from seeing each other after such a long time apart, but I can't risk losing your friendship just because of this sudden attraction."

"I don't know how sudden this is, at least on my end." He kissed her lips slightly and eased back. "I can't deny my desire for you, but I do promise not to do anything you don't want."

"I'm going to hold you to that," she told him. "I know this situation will be hard for you."

He laughed at her choice of wording. "You have no idea."

Three

Sliding a hand down the fitted satin bodice, Victoria stared at her reflection in the floor-to-ceiling mirror. The gown was perfect, and she was so thankful she'd made a handful of wedding dresses in her downtime just to keep on hand for when she decided to branch out and start a bridal line.

No one had seen any of the finished designs, but she'd told her mother where they were and to ship them all. Victoria had taken a couple apart and pieced them the way she wanted. Her mother had only grumbled and complained a little when she learned Victoria wouldn't be returning to L.A. before the wedding.

And that conversation was a whole different issue.

Of all the times she'd fantasized about her wedding day, both as a child and an adult, she'd never envisioned marrying Stefan under these extremely strange circumstances.

Yes, she'd pictured a few times how it would be if

they'd taken their friendship to another level. She wasn't too proud to admit that she'd fantasized his kisses a time or two…and that was *before* he'd taken her into his arms and captured her mouth, showing her exactly what she'd been missing all these years. How could she delete that arousing sensation from her memory? How could she get his taste from her lips?

And why would she want to erase such pleasure?

Because he was a playboy, and even though she believed him when he said he'd be faithful, that didn't stop his previous lovers from calling him.

So here she stood, confused, intrigued and ready to take a giant life-altering step toward marriage while two of Stefan's royal assistants adjusted the veil around her hair. Another assistant stood in front, touching up her blush and powder for at least the third time in an hour. Couldn't have the soon-to-be queen of Galini Isle looking peaked.

God, she sincerely hoped she didn't have to do this for every appearance as queen. Thankfully Stefan had assured her she wasn't required to do too much. Even though she was from an iconic Hollywood family, she didn't crave the limelight.

"Ladies, could I have a moment alone with my daughter?"

Victoria adjusted her gaze in the mirror to her mother, who stood just inside the arched doorway to one of the many suites in the royal palace.

Obviously comfortable with taking orders, the middle-aged ladies scurried away at Olivia's request. Once the door was closed, Olivia moved in behind Victoria and smiled.

"Are you sure this is what you want to do?"

Stamping down any doubts that rose deep within her, Victoria returned her mother's questioning smile. "I'm sure, Mom. Stefan needs me, and perhaps at this point in my life, I need him. He's my best friend."

"But in the past few years you've scarcely seen each other."

Victoria shrugged. "Distance doesn't matter. Not with us. You know we talk nearly every day, and it's nice to know I am the one he trusts. We have a bond, Mom. A bond stronger than most marriages, actually. This is just another chapter in our friendship. I was engaged for romantic love once. This time I'm doing it for another kind of love."

"That's what worries me, my darling." Olivia pulled the veil over Victoria's face, then placed her hands on her shoulders, giving a gentle squeeze. "As a mother I worry your heart will get mixed up in this. He's a wonderful man to you…as a friend. I worry that in the end Stefan will come out getting everything he wants and you will have just another heartache."

She'd hadn't told her mother she and Stefan had shared numerous scorching kisses. Opening up about that certainly wouldn't alleviate any worries. Best to keep some things private…especially until she could figure them out herself. Arousal and confusion combined made for a very shaky ground.

"I'm not worried at all," she assured her mother, knowing it wasn't completely a lie. "He's given me an open end to this marriage. I may love being queen or I may want to return to my life in L.A. once all this is over. We'll put in a few appearances once we're married and this will all seem legitimate. Neither of us will be hurt. We're both too strong to let this arrangement destroy us."

"You're fooling yourself if you think this will be that simple." Olivia tilted her head, quirking a brow. "I've seen Stefan's charm, Victoria. I've witnessed how he's looked at you since I arrived here. I've also taken notice how he's looked at you over the years. He's got an infatuation that I believe is beyond a friendship. There's no way the two of you can play house and not get tangled up in each other. He's one very attractive man. Lust clouds even the best of judgments."

Intrigued, Victoria wondered just what her mother saw over the years from Stefan. Lust? Desire? This past month had brought to light a deeper side to their relationship. Beyond the steamy kisses, Stefan had been attentive to each and every one of her needs. He'd had her favorite foods prepared, would bring her a freshly picked flower from the gardens as she was working, insisted on breaks to walk along the beach so she could relax. He'd been the prefect Prince Charming…all because he knew her better than she knew herself in some ways.

Victoria shook off the questions regarding just how deep Stefan's emotions were and the fact he'd made it perfectly clear he'd had thoughts of her as more than a friend.

"Mother, his appeal and his charm are nothing new to me. And no matter how you think he looks at me, I assure you we are only marrying for the sake of the country and to help launch my bridal line."

Though she knew from his promising kisses and honest words that was false. But since she was still reeling from that fact herself, that was another tidbit she'd keep inside. She had enough "what-ifs" swirling around in her mind without adding her mother's into the mix.

"Well, he'd be a fool not to think of you as more," Olivia retorted. "And since he's asked you to marry him, he's no fool. I've always wondered if the two of you would end up together. I can honestly say this is not how I'd envisioned it."

Nerves swirled around Victoria's stomach. As if having the title of princess weren't crazy and nerve wracking enough, she'd be sharing a bedroom with Stefan for months. There was no way to deny they had chemistry and no way she could lie to herself and say she hadn't replayed those kisses over and over.

Victoria turned away from the mirror, taking her mother's hands. "I'm going into this with my eyes wide open, Mom. With Alex I was blindsided, but Stefan isn't using me. He asked for my help at a time when there was no one else he could trust. And there's nothing that can damage my heart here because my heart isn't getting involved. Stefan won't hurt me."

Olivia looked as if she wanted to say something more, but Victoria squeezed her hands, unable to discuss this delicate topic any further with her mother. "Trust me."

With misty eyes full of worry, Olivia's gaze roamed over Victoria before she stepped back and sighed. "The last time I was at this castle I was playing a queen myself." She laughed. "I didn't even compare to how beautiful you look. Must be the difference between acting and real life. I can't believe how long ago that was."

Tears clogged her throat as Victoria hugged her mother, not caring about the crinkling of the silk fabrics.

"You were stunning in that film, Mom. Besides, I'm acting, too, aren't I? Playing queen for Stefan so his country will remain under his family's control. Ironic, isn't it? I always swore I'd never go into acting."

Olivia eased back, placing her hands over Victoria's bare shoulders. "You'll be queen for real, my darling. What happens inside the bedroom may not be real, but your title will be. Have you thought of that?"

As if she could think of little else.

Okay, well that was a lie. She'd thought immensely about the fact her fiancé/best friend had her stomach in knots. On one hand she was thrilled to be helping him obtain his goal as he helped with hers. She found herself admiring him for his determination to take what was rightfully his. Most other times she didn't think of him as a prince or king at all…and now, well, she thought of him as a man. A very sexy, very powerful man. Not powerful in the sense that he'd rule a country, but powerful in the sense that he'd dominate a room the moment he entered. He'd control any conversation, and he'd most certainly take charge in the bedroom.

And that path was precisely where her mind did not need to travel. She was letting her thoughts run rampant because of a few heated kisses. Very hot, very scorching, very toes-curling-in-her-stilettos kisses. Just because she'd once wondered "what-if," didn't mean that anything could stem from this arranged marriage. One day at a time is how she would have to approach this. She couldn't afford to let lust steal the greatest friendship she'd ever had.

But she knew her emotions were teetering on a precipice and it would take just a small nudge for Stefan to push her over the edge and right into his bed.

"Stefan and I have discussed everything, Mom." Victoria offered a comforting smile, hoping she wasn't lying to her mother. "I'm pretty sure we have this under control. He's assured me that he won't let me get in over my head. I'm basically an accessory for him at this point."

Accessory. She hated that term, but what else could a wife to one of the world's most powerful, sexy men be called? He didn't need her to do any public speaking or head up any charities, not in the short time they planned to be married, so the demeaning name, unfortunately, fit.

"I had to keep your brothers out of here, you know." Olivia stepped back, smoothing a hand down her raw silk, pale blue floor-length gown. "They insisted on making sure you were okay, so I had to assure them I'd check and report back."

Victoria laughed, turning to face the mirror and glance

at her reflection once more. "You can tell my self-imposed bodyguards that I am not having cold feet and I'm perfectly fine. They should be worrying about their wives standing up beside me in front of millions of people watching on TV. I swear, last I saw of Mia and Charlotte, they were so nervous I thought they were going to pass out."

"I'm going to see them now," Olivia said. "They will be fine, so I just want you to concentrate and worry about you. This is your day, no matter what the circumstances."

Olivia's hands cupped Victoria's shoulders as she laid her cheek against hers to look at their reflection in the mirror. "You're beautiful, Victoria. Stefan may change his mind about you having control in the end. He may not want to let you go once his title is secure."

"The Playboy Prince?" Victoria joked, using his nickname. "He'll let me go so he can shuffle back into the crowd of swooning women and place me back on that friend shelf."

Their kisses replayed once again in her mind. Could they go back to being just friends? Would she want them to? They hadn't even lived together for their allotted six months and already she had fantasized about taking those kisses further. How could she not? They were definite stepping stones to more promising, erotic things.

God, in heaven. What had she gotten herself into? She swore she wouldn't put her heart on the line again, but how could she not when Stefan needed her? Maybe she needed him, too. More than she ever realized.

Hundreds of guests filed through the grounds at Alexander Palace on the edge of the emerald ocean. Cameras were positioned at every angle to capture each moment as guests entered the Grand Ballroom. The world watched as the next king and queen of Galini Isle were about to wed in what the media had dubbed the most romantic wedding of the century. Obviously the mysterious bride angle had paid off.

Many of the headlines leading up to the nuptials had been amusing. Stefan's personal favorite: Playboy Prince Finally Settles Down.

The media could mock him all they wanted. He'd show them just how serious he was about this wedding…even if the idea of being wed scared the hell out of him.

He focused his eyes to the end of the aisle and his chest constricted, breath left his lungs.

Stefan couldn't think. At this moment, he couldn't even recall the exact reason he'd asked Victoria to marry him, but he was most thankful he had.

She floated—yes, floated—down the aisle like a glorious angel coming to rescue him, wearing an original-design gown that dipped just enough in the front to have his imagination running into overdrive, while still looking classy. Two strands of pearls draped over each of her toned biceps, hinting that they'd once been straps that a lover had slid off her slender shoulders. And damn if he didn't want to be that lover.

The dress cut perfectly into the curve of her waist and fell straight to the ground. A shimmery veil shielded her face, and Stefan couldn't wait to lift it, to kiss his bride and get another taste of the flavor he'd come to crave from her lips.

Stefan knew his best friend was a walking fantasy that every man would give his last dying breath for. Well, except for that bastard she'd been engaged to. Stefan straightened his shoulders and smiled. He hoped the jerk was watching his TV and regretting letting such an amazingly talented, beautiful woman out of his life.

Victoria's gaze met his, and Stefan's heart clenched as

a wide smile spread across her face from behind the iridescent veil.

"You've chosen a beautiful queen, Stefan. Victoria is perfect."

Stefan merely nodded at his brother's whispered compliment. Mikos Alexander stood as best man, and Stefan knew his brother breathed a sigh of relief when he'd discovered the country would remain under the Alexander name. Stefan had worried when his brother had married a divorcée, thus preventing him from claiming the throne, but Victoria was a perfect fit.

Never in his life would he forget how she'd stepped up to save him, selflessly and radiantly. Stefan moved forward, taking Victoria's hands in his.

She squeezed them before turning to the priest. In a blur their vows were said and the gold heirloom rings exchanged. As Stefan lifted her veil, Victoria chewed on her bottom lip as if nerves were getting the best of her.

"You may kiss your bride."

Stefan wasted no time in capturing Victoria's lips. Though he couldn't claim her mouth the way he wanted to, considering there were television cameras on them and millions of people watching to see how the Playboy Prince would act, he was still just as affected by that one, tender kiss as he had been when they'd been alone on his balcony and shared their first passionate encounter. He'd taken every opportunity since then to steal more…each one always sweeter than the last and leaving him wanting.

Easing her soft lips from his, Victoria's gaze landed on his. "Good thing we've been practicing," she whispered with a slight grin.

He smiled and placed a quick peck on her lips once more before taking her hand and turning to the crowd.

"I present to you Prince and Princess Alexander," the priest exclaimed. "Galini Isle's next king and queen."

Applause broke out and Stefan glanced toward Victoria's family seated in the front row. Her brothers were smiling, but a hint of caution clouded their eyes, and her mother, the grand Hollywood icon, had unshed tears and a smile on her face...a face full of worry.

Stefan couldn't feel any guilt right now. How could he? He was going to be king and Victoria was going to stand by his side. Finally he could explore his feelings further because while he knew he wanted to be with her in more than just a friendly way, he also wasn't sure just how much of a commitment he could offer after the six months if she decided to remain in their marriage. He did, after all, get his reputation for a reason.

Right now, though, he had to concentrate on his title and gaining his country's confidence by eliminating the black mark over his family's name. That was his first order of business. But seducing Victoria would certainly be a welcome distraction, even if a challenge, and one he couldn't turn down. Especially now that he'd had more than a few tastes.

As he and his new bride made their way back up the aisle, Stefan beamed knowing he'd just married the most beautiful, intelligent, sexy woman. And for the next six months, and maybe even more if she chose to stay, Victoria was not only his best friend, she was his wife...and possibly lover.

Arousal shot through him. He wasn't known as the Playboy Prince for nothing. Seduction had always been his partner in crime.

Victoria had never smiled so much in all her thirty-two years combined as she had tonight. Between the professional royal photo shoot with Stefan's brother and wife and Victoria's family and then of the two of them alone, then the grand parade after the ceremony where they were shown off through the entire seaside town, she'd almost convinced herself this was real.

Now they were at the reception back inside the grand ballroom of the palace, and Stefan held her in his arms as they danced their first dance as Prince and Princess Alexander.

The spacious room with high, stained-glass ceilings had been transformed from the ceremony and set up to host the reception in the hours they'd been gone for the traditional wedding parade.

A dance floor had appeared surrounded by elegant white silk draped between tall, thick columns. White silk also adorned each table, as did slender crystal vases with a spray of white flowers and clear glass beads in each.

Thousands of twinkling lights created a magical, fairy-tale theme. Ice sculptures and champagne fountains were in abundance. The ballroom had shifted into something from a dream and something fit for royalty.

And while so much beauty surrounded her, she couldn't think of anything else but the man in her arms. Her doubts, her confusion, it all slid into the very back of her mind as the slow, classical ballad played and she swayed against him.

His warmth, his familiar masculine scent and the powerful hold he had on her all made her want to put her head on his shoulder and relish the moment. So she did. He'd held her numerous times over the years. But she knew in her heart this time was different.

With a sigh, she closed her eyes, letting him lead in their dance, and rested her head just for a moment on one broad, muscular shoulder. The man was the proverbial good time, but right now she wanted to just lean on him, to draw from his strength and courage.

Her cheek rested against his smooth, silky sash. Victoria had known he'd wear his best royal dress for the ceremony, but her Prince Charming had truly been a sight to see, waiting at the end of the white-petal-covered aisle. It wasn't often in their years together she saw him in person dressed as a prince. Normally they were just hanging out in casual clothes. But with his tailored black suit with shiny gold double-breasted buttons, glossy black shoes, and a wide, blue sash crossing from shoulder to opposite hip, he exuded bad-boy prince. She knew beneath all the impressive gold buttons and fringe-capped shoulders lay a great deal of body art molding over and around his chiseled arms, chest and back. Sexy didn't even begin to describe her man.

Medals, which stemmed from charity work to his family's crest and various other ranks, also adorned one side of his jacket. The blue from his sash matched his eyes perfectly, and he couldn't look more fit for a royal role than if he were the star in one of her brothers' films.

The designer in her should've made notes on how well the lines were cut in his suit, but the woman in her was too busy admiring the view. Hey, he may be her best friend, but he was still one magnificently built man and she'd be a fool not to notice. But she'd been noticing more and more in the past month leading up to their nuptials. Was she getting caught up in the wedding, or was she beginning to see him as more of a man? He'd always been charming, but recently he'd become…irresistible. And her desire for him was starting to consume her.

The glamorous ceremony was something she'd remember for the rest of her life. With celebrities, other royalty and every media outlet on hand to snap thousands of pictures, the scene was something out of a modern-day fairy tale.

"You made a beautiful bride, Victoria," he murmured. "I'm one lucky prince."

She raised her head, looked him in the eyes and smiled. "Oh, I'm pretty lucky, too. I'm living every little girl's dream by marrying royalty and living in a palace."

"Only for two weeks," he reminded her. "After our honeymoon phase, we'll travel to L.A. I'm anxious to see you at work and visit with your family. It's grown considerably since I was there last."

"I'm anxious to get back, too, but I don't mind playing hooky. Not when I'm living a fantasy life."

"Speaking of fantasy," he murmured, raking his eyes down to where her cleavage nestled against his tux. "Have I told you how amazing you look today?"

"You're letting your reputation take over," she joked, though nerves danced in her belly at the hunger in his eyes. "My eyes are up here."

"Oh, I know where your eyes are." He smiled, meeting her gaze. "But I'm enjoying the entire view of my beautiful bride."

He wanted her and he wasn't hinting anymore, which only made her even more intrigued.

Obviously the ball was in her court. Game on.

"And my reputation has nothing to do with what I'm feeling right now." He pulled her body closer to his as he spun her in a wide circle around the perimeter of the dance floor. "Trust me, I'm the envy of every man around the world. I nearly swallowed my tongue when you came down the aisle."

"As a designer, I take that as a compliment." She laughed. "As a woman, I'm thrilled to know I have that effect on someone."

He shifted slightly against her, a wicked smile on his face. "Oh, I'm not unaffected."

Mercy. No, he wasn't. How had this dance gotten so far out of control? And why did she care? How could she avoid the fact Stefan was so open with his feelings? Should she even attempt to hide that she'd been thinking of him in a new light, as well? Those "what-if" thoughts from years ago were now more realistic and...obtainable.

Did she dare try to move to the next level with Stefan? The idea made her nervous and excited and, most of all, curious. All of her giddy emotions overshadowed the fear and doubts.

Their wedding night was fast approaching. Only hours until the reception drew to a close and they would be alone. Perfect timing?

Well played, Fate. Well played.

"You're blushing again," he told her, stealing a quick kiss. "I know everyone is watching us and the cameras are still rolling, but that kiss was purely selfish. I'm finding it hard to keep my hands off you, Victoria."

"Stefan." Her heart beat against his chest. "I'm not sure...I mean, yes, I'm finding myself more drawn to you than just as a friend, but won't taking another step here make this arrangement more complicated?"

"We won't know unless we try," he told her, nipping at her lips again. "I'd hate to let an opportunity pass me by. What if sleeping together is the best decision we ever made?"

"Is that where we're headed?" she asked, already knowing what he'd say.

Unfortunately, she kept hearing her mother's warning about getting her heart entangled in this man. Fortunately her heart had already been trampled and crushed, so there was no more to break. And she knew Stefan would never hurt her.

"How much longer are we staying?" she asked as the orchestra slowed the song down toward the end.

He smiled. "Anxious to get me all alone?"

Considering they'd known each other for so long and he knew her better than most people, he had a love for his family that rivaled her own and his loyalty to his country made her heart melt, she may have a little trouble avoiding his charms.

Oh, the hell with it. Why dance around this attraction? Six months of torture would be pure…well, torture. People did friends with benefits all the time, right? Granted she never had, but Stefan was special and he so obviously wanted her, which was good because she couldn't deny it any longer.

"Maybe I am," she told him with a grin, knowing she was playing with fire.

As the song ended, he pulled her close, close enough she could feel just how turned on he was, and whispered in her ear, "I've been waiting for you to say that. What do you say we go start on our honeymoon?"

And with that thrilling promise, he tugged on her hand and they slipped through the crowd and out the double doors.

Four

As he led her through the long, marble hallways, Victoria didn't care about the doubts and fears swirling around in her head, nor did she care about the fact she'd just left hundreds of guests in the main ballroom.

What she did care about was how much farther they had to go until they reached their destination because she wanted Stefan, and the realization of just how much she wanted him both thrilled and scared her. This sexual tension had been brewing before she'd come to Galini Isle a month ago—there had to have been an underlying current or she wouldn't have been so eager to have his mouth on hers when they'd shared their first kiss…or the several scorchers that followed.

But she couldn't think about anything from their past now or she'd remember that this man was her best friend… and he was about to become her lover. Something about taking their relationship to a level of intimacy aroused her even more. She could analyze later all the reasons this wasn't a wise move…but right now she didn't care. She. Wanted. Him.

When Stefan pulled her through a set of heavy double doors, she blinked into the darkness, trying to get her bearings, and wondered if they'd just entered his master suite.

His room was on this floor, but she'd thought it was farther down the wing. She'd been in his suite a few times, but for purely innocent reasons…as opposed to now, when the reason was a bit more naughty.

She remembered his king-size bed with navy silk sheets. The bed had always sat in the middle of his suite, dominating the room.

A man like Stefan with his bad-boy behavior wouldn't have something as boring as a bed in a corner. He'd want that bed and all the action taking place there to be center stage.

Stefan eased the door shut and with a swift click, slid the lock into place. He immediately set the lights to a soft glow.

Good, that would help her nerves if she didn't have to have spotlights on her. While Stefan had seen her in swimsuits, he'd never seen her fully naked—not for lack of his playful trying at times, but she'd always written off his silly remarks as jokes. Had there been genuine want behind his words?

Victoria turned around, amazed at the room spread out before her, and she laughed. This was his idea of a romantic wedding night? Stefan never failed to amaze and surprise her.

"If someone starts looking for us, they'd check my wing first," Stefan told her. He slid off his jacket, flinging it to the side without taking his eyes off her as he stalked— yes, stalked—right toward her. "They'd never think to look in the theater."

How many women had he snuck into this room or any other room in this magnificent palace, for that matter? She knew the media really exploited his bachelor status and the fact that he enjoyed women, but she also knew most of their accounts were accurate. Stefan never made any apologies for the man he was, and that's perhaps why people loved him so much. He was honest to a fault and sinfully charming.

Past women didn't matter to her. He was her husband now, and what he did before this moment was ridiculous for her to even entertain. She wasn't a virgin, and they weren't committing themselves to anything permanent. They were adults, best friends, and they were acting on these newfound sexual feelings. So why analyze it to death when there was one hot, sexy, aroused prince standing before her looking like he wanted to devour her? No woman would be stupid enough to turn that invitation down... especially from her own husband.

Wedding night or not, this would be one experience she'd never forget. She needed the awkwardness and doubts to get out of her mind because she wanted to concentrate on the here and now.

"You look beautiful." He closed the gap between them, running a fingertip along her exposed collarbone. Shivers coursed through her at his provocative, simple touch. "The way this dress molds to your body makes me wonder if you could possibly fit anything between this satin and your skin."

Her eyes roamed over his bronzed face and his heavy-lidded eyes as his finger continued to tickle its way back and forth across her collarbone, teasing her, tempting her. If one finger had that much of an impact on her senses, who knew what a full-bodied touch would do.

"I'm a designer," she told him, reaching up to slide one

button at a time through the hole of his dress shirt. "It's my job to make things fit and create an illusion of perfection."

His hands glided down her arms, slid to her hips and tugged her until she was pelvis to pelvis with him. Chills raced over her body, the promise of what was to come making her shiver.

"I'd say fitting won't be a problem, and there's no illusion." His gaze dropped to her lips, to her breasts pressed against his chest and back up to her face. "There's plenty of perfection without the tricks you may practice as a designer. I've known you for years, Tori, and there's nothing imperfect about you."

The attack on her mouth was fierce and oh so welcoming. The man knew what he wanted, and the fact that he wanted her made her feel alive again for the first time in months. Maybe that made her shallow, but she needed to feel beautiful, sexy and, yes, even needed.

Stefan may be her best friend, but right now she wasn't having thoughts of friendship. Desire shot through her as she pressed her body against his.

How many times had she kissed him, hugged him? How could she have taken for granted such a hard body?

Victoria eased back, continuing her work on his shirt. Stefan slid her hands away and pulled it over his head, ignoring the last few buttons that weren't undone.

That chest. She'd seen it many times before, but she hadn't seen this fresh ink and his finely sculpted body in some time. Victoria glided her hands up over his chiseled abs and outlined the new tattoo over one of his pecs.

"How come every time I see you, you have new ink?" she murmured, tracing the detailed dragon.

"I like the art," he said simply. "Let's discuss tattoos later. How the hell do I get you out of this thing on your head and this dress without hurting one of us?"

Victoria laughed, thankful he'd lightened the mood. This is what she needed. The playful side of Stefan. The side that always made her smile. Of course, she had a feeling he'd be showing her another side that would make her smile even more in a minute.

She reached up, sliding several pins from her hair and placing them on the counter along the wall. After removing the diamond tiaralike headband and veil, she laid it out along the counter, as well.

She realized she was taking her time. In part she wanted this moment to last. But she also couldn't help being a little afraid of where this epic step would take them.

"I wish I'd designed a dress that could just peel off," she told him, reaching behind her. "But I'm afraid there's a zipper, and you're going to have to get it."

She turned, giving him her back but throwing him a glance over her shoulder. "Sorry I wasn't thinking ahead."

"Oh, this is my pleasure," he told her with a crooked smile and a wink.

When his fingers came up to her back and slid to the zipper, she couldn't suppress the shiver that raced through her. Arousal quickly overrode her awkwardness and doubts that threatened to creep in.

As the material parted in the back, Victoria shimmied her arms slightly so the dress fell down the front of her, leaving her standing in a strapless bustier that lifted her meager chest into something voluptuous and enticing…at least she hoped that's how he saw her.

Stefan didn't know which god deserved credit for making Victoria realize that the two of them sleeping together wasn't a mistake, but he'd graciously drop to his knees and thank him.

"Oh," he whispered when she turned around. "Had I

known you looked that good, I would've insisted you go without the dress during the ceremony."

Just as he'd hoped, Victoria laughed. That rich, seductive sound washed over him. As much as his body wanted hers, he also wanted her to be comfortable. He couldn't allow any uneasiness to settle between them.

"This royal wedding would've been talked about until the end of time," she joked. "Besides, since I'm the designer, I would've looked rather strange coming down the aisle without a gown."

"Strange?" he asked, tracing the top of the silk material that covered her tan breasts. "No. Sexy as hell and the fantasy of every man? Absolutely."

Victoria bit her lip but held his gaze.

"Don't," he told her. "Don't think. Don't worry. Just… feel."

She shivered beneath his touch, and Stefan wished she knew the effect she had on him was just as potent. He had shivers racing through his body just thinking of what they were about to do. God, he'd waited so long to make love to her and here they were.

Of course, all those times he'd envisioned them sleeping together, he never once pictured her in a wedding dress beforehand.

She inhaled, causing her chest to press deeper into his touch. The rustling of the dress had him pulling back just enough so she could step out of it.

"One of us still has too many clothes on." She smiled, picking up her dress, and, with great care, she laid it over the back of one of the oversized leather theater chairs. "Normally you're so eager to show off your body. Are you getting stage fright, Prince Alexander?"

A naughty smile spread across her face. She was literally a sinful sight before him, but he'd never been known for being a choir boy.

"Oh, I'm not afraid of anything." He wasted no time in stripping down to his black boxer briefs. "I was merely admiring the view of my sexy new wife."

When Victoria's eyes raked down his body, pausing at his throbbing erection, then back up to meet his eyes, she bit her lip. Nerves were getting to her and he refused to let her overthink this.

"You were starting to relax. Come on, Tori." He reached out, sliding his hands up her bare arms and stepping into her. "You've seen me in swimming trunks skimpier than this."

Her eyes locked on to his, her hands coming up to rest on his chest. "True, but this is so much different. I just don't want this to change us…you know, afterward."

He kissed her lips, gently, slowly. Kissed his way along her jawline, down the long, slender column of her throat, pleased when she tilted her head back and groaned. He'd dreamed of this moment for so long. Longer than he liked to admit, even to himself. He'd never allowed any woman to have such control over his mind or his fantasies.

"Nothing will change," he assured her between kisses. "Unless it's better. And I'm positive in the next few minutes, things between us will get a whole lot better."

Victoria's arms circled around his neck as her head turned, her mouth colliding with his.

And that's when the dam burst. His, hers. Did it matter? He'd wanted her for years, and whether she'd wanted him that long or she'd just decided it in the past few weeks they'd been together he didn't know, but he did know he was going to have her. Now. Here.

Stefan encircled her waist with his hands, slid them on down to the slight flare of her hips and slowly walked her to the bar in the back of the room. When he hoisted her up onto to the counter, she laughed.

"In a hurry?" she mocked with a teasing grin.

"I've waited for this for a long time," he told her, staring at her moist, swollen lips. "I always swore if we ever came to this moment I'd take my time. But right now I can't wait another minute."

Her smiled weakened as she held his gaze. "I think I've been waiting for this for a long time, too. I just never realized…"

Stefan didn't want a confession, not now. He didn't want her to explore her feelings…or, God forbid, try to uncover his. He just wanted Victoria.

He stepped between her gloriously spread legs, slid his palms up her smooth, bare thighs and thumbed along the edge of her white silk panties.

When she hooked her thumbs through the thin straps and shifted from side to side to ease them off, he gratefully helped her slide them down her long, toned legs.

She reached around behind the bustier.

"Leave it," he ordered. "I like how you look right now."

With tousled hair, bare skin from the waist down and that white silk bustier molded to her curves and pushing her breasts up…yeah, he liked her just the way she was. All sexy and rumpled and ready for him.

"I want to feel your skin on mine," she told him, still working on the back of her lingerie.

How could he argue with her defense? No man with air in his lungs would turn down bare breasts.

"Then let me help," he offered.

He eased his hands around and, one by one, each hook-and-eye closure popped open. Thankfully it was cut low, so there weren't very many. When the garment was fully open, he stepped back.

Victoria held on to the front of the material still covering her breasts. "You're sure?" she asked.

Without a word, he brushed her hands aside, took the bustier and threw it over his shoulder. And finally, she was completely and utterly naked. And completely and utterly his.

He palmed one breast in each hand as he captured her lips once more. Arching her back, Victoria leaned into his touch, his kiss, and let out a soft, low groan.

Her arms came around his shoulders, her fingertips toying with the ends of his hair on the nape of his neck. She shifted, scooting to the edge of the counter, and wrapping her legs around his waist. Stefan let go of her breasts long enough to shuck his boxers and kick them to the side. With her legs around him, he palmed her backside and lifted her off the bar until she was settled right above him.

His eyes searched hers as he walked a few steps to the nearest wall, where he rested her back. He stayed still, waiting for any hint of a signal that she was uncomfortable or not ready to go through with this.

Stopping would kill him, but even with his hormones in overdrive he'd stop if she said the word. But when he looked in her eyes, all he saw was desire. Heavy lids, half-covered vibrant blue eyes…eyes that were focused on his lips.

At the same time he sealed his mouth to hers, he slid her down to take him fully. The flood of emotions within him was indescribable. Her body all around his, the soft feel of her skin, the fresh, floral aroma and her tiny little gasps had him nearly embarrassing himself and drawing their first encounter to an abrupt, climactic halt.

He moved within her, slowly, then, when her hips rocked faster, he increased the pace.

She tore her lips from his. "Please."

If she liked things fast and sweaty, they could very well kill each other before the six months were up because she was speaking his language.

Victoria gripped his shoulders, flung her head back and closed her eyes. That long column of her neck begged to be licked, savored. He nibbled his way up, then back down and nestled his face between her breasts.

"Stefan…."

Yeah, he knew. She was close, which was a relief because so was he. He normally prided himself on his stamina, but one touch from Victoria and he was ready to explode. He didn't take the time or the energy to think that this had never happened before. There was something about his Tori….

Her legs tightened around his waist as her whole body stiffened. He grabbed her face, forced her to look at him and for the briefest of seconds, when their eyes met, he felt a twinge of something he didn't recognize. But he certainly wasn't taking the time to figure it out, not when he had a sexy, wild woman bucking in his arms, finding her release.

Capturing her lips while she came undone around him was all he wanted. His tongue slid in and out, mimicking their bodies. His own release built and before he knew it he, too, let go. He gave in to Victoria's sweet body, allowing her to take him—her welcoming arms enveloping him and her soft words calming him.

Never had he experienced anything like this before. But he knew that the next several months with his best friend-turned-wife would be nothing if not life-altering.

And that epiphany scared the hell out of him.

Victoria sat in the oversize cozy leather chair in the palace theater waiting for the movie to start and eating from a tub of popcorn. Only moments ago the man beside her rocked her world in a way she hadn't known possible, and now he pretended as if their giant step beyond friendship were perfectly normal.

After they'd nearly killed each other in a bout of heated, frenzied sex, she'd thrown on his tux shirt instead of her gown. He'd slipped back into his pants, leaving his gloriously tanned and tattooed chest bare. He nearly had a whole sleeve of tats on one sculpted arm. The swirls slid over his shoulder and stretched from his back over his pecs. And Victoria wanted to trace every line, every detail with her fingertip, then follow with her tongue.

God, he'd turned her into a sex fiend. Knowing Stefan, that had been his goal all along.

Who knew he had such…skills. Well, given the amount of women the paparazzi put him with over the years, she should've known, but she'd not thought of his hidden talents before. Shame that.

But she'd be thinking of them now. She had a feeling they would be in the forefront of her mind for quite some time. Would she ever get used to seeing, touching her best friend in such a way?

"So do we talk about this or just watch the movie?" she asked, reaching into the giant tub of popcorn he'd prepared.

He propped his feet upon the footrest of his own oversized leather chair and threw her a smile. "I knew you wouldn't be able to just relax and watch the movie."

Relax? After what had just happened? Her body was still trembling and her orgasm had stopped twenty minutes ago. Yeah, definite skills. But even through the climax-induced haze, she had to know what he was thinking. She didn't care if that was too girly and mushy for him, she couldn't just pretend this moment hadn't changed her life.

"Do you feel different?" she asked, turning in her chair to face him.

A wicked grin spread across his handsome, devilish face. "Oh, yeah."

With a playful swat on his arm, she laughed. "Stefan, be serious. We're married and we just had sex."

"Just sex?" he asked, quirking one black brow.

Images of how they must've looked slammed into her. His golden, toned body plastering hers against the wall as she arched into his touch. Her glorious Greek prince staking his claim, dominating her.

"Okay, so it was amazing sex," she admitted as tingles continued to spread through her. "This isn't going to be weird now, is it? Because I really can't handle weird."

"The way you were groaning earlier and the way you're smiling now, I'd say you feel anything but weird."

Victoria rolled her eyes. "You're begging for compliments, aren't you? I already said it was great sex. I just don't want this to get uncomfortable between us."

He reached out, grabbed her hand and squeezed. "I care for you just as much as I always have," he assured her, all joking gone from his face. "You're still my best friend, but I've discovered that my best friend has a kick-ass body that I can't wait to take my time in savoring and getting to know better."

Chills and excitement coursed through her at his promise. If he was this confident, than why was she letting fear spread through her? Why borrow trouble when she'd just had the most incredible sexual experience of her life?

"I think this marriage is going to be one of the wisest decisions we ever made," she told him.

As the movie started on the screen, Stefan held on to her hand, occasionally stroking his thumb across her skin. The man had a tender side, and he wasn't afraid to express himself. They'd held hands before, but holding them after being so intimate took on a whole new meaning.

If the next six months of their marriage were anything like tonight, she'd certainly think twice about walking away. She may just be queen of Galini Isle forever.

"You picked my favorite movie," she told him as the title popped up on the screen. "You had this whole night planned, didn't you?"

He shrugged and grinned. "I actually had the movie planned because I thought you'd want to get back some sense of normalcy after the circus today. The sex was just a major added bonus."

"Oh, you have such pretty words," she mocked with a heavy sigh. "Watch it, Stefan, I may not find it in my heart to leave you after six months."

And while she was joking on the outside, inside her heart she feared she may have gotten in deeper than even she thought she would go.

Five

Victoria stood over the mahogany desk and sighed as she stared down at the scattered dress designs and random doodles. She'd started fresh sketches the day after her wedding and now, over a week later, she still wasn't happy with the results.

Nothing compared to her own lavish gown…of which many replicas were already being made by designers who only wished they would have had the initial idea.

And while that dress was her absolute favorite, Victoria didn't want to re-create it for resale. That unique design was hers, whether the marriage was real or not. She wanted to keep the gown special, but she would do others that were similar for future clients. And she knew she couldn't stop other designers from trying to mimic her gown, but they still wouldn't be the same. Hers was literally one of a kind.

Her thoughts circled back around to the "real" marriage.

She didn't know why she always put quotations around the word in her head. Her marriage to Stefan was as real as anyone else's marriage. In fact, she'd bet her entire year's salary that theirs was better than the majority of those living in Hollywood because she sincerely loved Stefan and would do anything for him...obviously a point she'd proven.

Not only did they share that bond and connection of their friendship, but the sexual chemistry was beyond amazing. Didn't married couples complain that after they said "I do" the light burned out on the passion? Yeah, there was no dimming the desire in the bedroom here.

After their initial lovemaking in the theater—and their movie night—Stefan had brought her into his master suite where they'd playfully undressed each other once again and enjoyed the benefits of the sunken garden tub in his master bath.

If this was how the whole friends-with-benefits thing worked, no wonder so many people jumped on board. Six months of Stefan attending to her intimate needs hadn't been part of the initial bargain, but it had become a surprising extra.

Unfortunately, her emotions were a jumbled mess. She had been stunned at what an attentive, passionate lover Stefan was, but when she started really thinking about their intimacy, she couldn't help but feel they'd passed the point of no return. After this six months, if she chose to leave, could they actually go back to just being friends?

Victoria turned her focus back to the pencil sketches staring up at her. Before her wedding she would've loved these designs, but now that she was technically a princess—still an odd term to grasp when referring to herself—she wished for all of her future brides to feel the same on their special day.

She wanted to launch her Fairy-tale Collection with magnificent gowns that women would love just as much as the one she wore, and if she was going to start this, she needed to stop coming up with garbage.

Raking her hands through her hair, she groaned.

"Bad time?"

She spun in the direction of the door to find Stefan entering their bedroom. In the past she'd always appreciated his fine build, but now that she'd seen, tasted and touched every delicious inch, she had a whole new admiration for her sexy husband…a weird sensation to associate with Stefan, but surprisingly a very welcome one.

Would it be too taboo for the prince to walk around naked? A shame, really, to cover such a magnificent creature.

If one didn't know he was a prince, they'd never guess from his attire. Though he did look mighty fine in his black T-shirt stretched over his broad shoulders and faded, designer jeans, it was the baseball cap pulled low to shield his face that captured her attention. Not often had she seen him in a hat, but he wore it well. And while he may look very American with his ensemble, he was every bit the Greek god she knew him to be.

"Perfect timing, actually." She turned away from her ghastly drawings and leaned back on the desk. "What's up?"

Those long legs ate up the space between them, and he rested a hip beside hers on the desk. "Well, I'm in the honeymoon phase and my wife is working. The tradition in my country is that these two weeks are for the husband and wife to get to know each other."

Wife. She didn't know if she'd ever get used to that term coming from Stefan's lips…especially when referring to her.

Victoria laughed. "I'm pretty sure we know each other quite well."

He reached around, fingering through her designs. "Still drawing random sketches?" he asked.

"Yeah. It's always easier to concentrate when I'm doodling and just let my mind relax."

He lifted a torn piece of scratch paper. "This looks like my family crest, but…are those initials?"

Victoria nodded. "I intertwined our initials together. Silly, isn't it?"

"Amazing how you're so extremely talented and still hard on yourself."

He took her hands in his and flashed a wicked smile. "Let's get out of here. Go down to the beach or have a picnic. Want to go for a ride on my new bike?"

"Is that a double entendre?" she asked, smiling. "How about we take a ride on the bike to the beach for a picnic?"

"And you'll lay off work the rest of the day?" he asked.

She watched him, those taut muscles beneath his shirt, the way the hat shielded those cobalt-colored eyes. As his best friend she hadn't been able to deny him anything, so as his wife and lover she definitely couldn't say no.

"Just today," she promised. "I really do need to get this line started, and these designs are crap right now."

Stefan pulled her up as he stood. "All the more reason you need a break. I know how you get when you're frustrated. Nothing will make you happy until you take a breather, refocus and come back to it. Besides, you're not sleeping well and I know it's because of work."

She jerked back. "How do you know I'm not sleeping well?"

"Because you normally snore like a train," he laughed. "All you've been doing lately is tossing and turning."

"I do not snore," she told him with a tilt of her chin. "You're lying."

He hugged her closer and nuzzled her neck. "Maybe I'm not wearing you out enough before bed."

The familiar masculine aroma that she always associated with him enveloped her. Amazing how their time apart didn't hinder his knowledge of how she worked. They may not see each other in person as often as she would've liked, but he still knew every layer to her. Even more so now since they'd slept together.

"If you want to ride my bike, in any form of the term, let me offer myself to your services."

Victoria laughed, smacking his shoulder. "I'm so glad you're willing to sacrifice yourself for my work."

With a loud smack, he kissed her on the lips. "Anything for my new bride."

"Let me change and I'll meet you in the kitchen."

His hand snaked up her shirt, his thumb skimming the edge of her lacy bra. "Do you need help changing?"

His touch affected her in ways she'd never known before, and she had to assume the chills and instant erotic pleasure that came from his fingertips stemmed from their playful, yet intense lovemaking.

"What I need is for you to get that picnic lunch prepared so we can go," she told him, swatting his hand away and taking a step back.

He shoved his hands in his jean pockets and smiled… Oh, the things that smile did to her insides, touching places she had thought dead since her exploited and humiliating breakup months ago.

She had known Stefan would be there to help her through the tough time, she just never imagined it would be with their clothes off.

Every time she thought of how fast, how thrilling their

new relationship was, nerves settled low in her belly. She was already getting too comfortable and she hadn't even put a dent in this six-month period.

Even though he'd given her control in the end, she couldn't help but wonder if he'd tire of her, physically, by then and if he'd be eager to get back to his old, playboy ways.

"I already had my chef prepare the food," he told her. "How soon can you be ready?"

"I'm just going to throw on some jeans and a tank."

Stefan rolled his eyes. "You are a fashion designer. You never 'throw on' anything. You'll go to the closet and think about it, try something on, discard it and start over."

Offended that he'd hit the nail on the head, she folded her arms over her chest. "For your information, I know exactly what I'm going to wear."

He quirked a brow and tilted his head. "Really? Then I'll just wait."

In her mind she went through everything she'd brought from the States. She hadn't had all of her things shipped since they were returning to L.A. after the two-week honeymoon period was over, so her options were limited.

"You're just waiting to see me naked," she joked, heading to her walk-in closet.

"An added perk," he agreed. "But I want to see you get ready as fast as you claim you can. This will be a first."

Victoria eyed her selection. If they were riding a bike, she would need pants, so she grabbed her favorite pair of designer jeans. Her eyes roamed up to the top rack of clothes where she'd hung her shirts. A little sleeveless emerald-green wrap shirt caught her eye—perfect. Sexy, cool and comfortable. She glanced to the shoe rack at the end of the closet and grabbed her gold strappy sandals. Not bike material, but perfect for the picnic and beach.

"Voilà," she announced, holding her items up in the air as she came from the closet, then stopped.

The man was lying across the bed wearing nothing but tattoos and a grin. He'd taken off his hat, too, leaving his hair messy and those cobalt eyes, beneath heavy lids, staring across the room at her.

"You don't fight fair," she told him, trying to remain in place and not attack her husband like some overeager teenager.

"Fighting wasn't on my mind at all." He laced his hands behind his head, forcing his muscles to flex beautifully beneath his tats. "Looks like you still need to undress."

Check and mate. And by the smirk on his face, he knew he had her. He'd played this scene perfectly.

How could she turn down such a blatant invitation? Even with their short time frame looming in her mind, she couldn't deny herself giving and receiving his pleasure.

She tossed her items to the floor, not caring where they landed. In a slow, what she hoped was sexy, striptease, she loosened the ties on her shirt and flung it off to the side, as well.

"Since I'm being rushed, I may need some help," she told him, sliding her thumbs into her jeans and sending them to puddle at her feet. She stepped out and smiled when his eyes roamed over her body...twice. "You want the job?"

"Sure, I'll help by getting you out of these."

He came to stand, all six-foot-plus glorious inches of him. He was beautifully tanned, magnificent and, for now, he was hers.

"Being with you like this should be awkward." She reached out, tracing his family's crest he had tattooed over his heart. "But it's not. I'm amazed how comfortable I've been being intimate with you."

"You're not going to want to leave me at the end of this six months," he joked, sliding the strap of her bra down one arm.

She reached around, unhooking the unwanted garment, and smiled. "Maybe not. We may just like being married to each other. This is the best relationship I've ever been in."

"You're just saying that to get me into bed," he told her, his hands coming up to cup her breasts.

"Yes, because it is so hard to get you naked and horny." She laughed.

The corners of his mouth kicked up at the same time he scooped her up and tossed her onto the bed. She bounced once before he was on her, pinning her hands above her head.

"I don't know why, but that smart mouth of yours has always been one of the things I love most about you."

She knew he loved her the way best friends loved each other, but when he said it like that, especially now that they were practically naked, the words sounded a bit more intimate and almost…awkward. She so did not want awkwardness to enter into this marriage or friendship. She enjoyed this friends-with-benefits arrangement they had. Her heart couldn't handle any more.

"You're thinking," he murmured, looking down. "None of that here. Work and everything else stays out of this bed."

She smiled, knowing he was the proverbial "fun guy," but he also knew when to be serious and when to work. The media had just caught him mostly in those "fun guy" moments.

But she knew the man beneath the playboy persona.

"Not thinking right now is perfect," she told him, looping her arms around his neck. "Marrying you was good for my creative mind."

He laughed. "Let me show you how creative I can be."

Six

Stefan's cell went off again. And again, he ignored it.

"Whoever is calling you must want you pretty bad," Victoria told him. "Why don't you just answer it?"

Because he wanted to ignore the fact that certain people did not believe this marriage was real and that he was officially off the market.

"Could be important," she went on as she slid her dainty feet back into her sandals and strapped them around her ankles.

After an intense bout of sex, a ride on his bike and a picnic at the beach, the last thing he wanted was an interruption to the day—especially by answering phone calls from past lovers. He had his best friend-turned-wife with him, and he was happier than he'd been in a long time. All of his goals were within his reach, and he didn't want anything to dampen his mood.

He'd promised Tori he'd be faithful, and he wasn't going

back on his word. Never before had he promised to be exclusive, something he made sure his lovers knew up front, but with Tori warming his bed, he didn't mind at all. He kept waiting for that feeling of being trapped to overtake him, but so far he'd not felt anything but complete and utter happiness.

"They'll leave a message," he told her, not really caring if they did or not.

Victoria leaned her hands back in the sand, shook her head and allowed her hair to fall past her shoulders and cascade down her back. As her gaze settled on the emerald waters before them, he smiled. It wasn't every man who could say he married his best friend…a hot, sexy, centerfold-material friend. Damn, he'd lucked out. An open-ended marriage was absolutely the way to go. Once the crown was his in a few months, he'd seriously have everything: title of king and Victoria in his bed with no major commitment to marriage.

And hopefully he could also convince her brothers to work with him on a documentary to clear his father's name.

"I'm not jealous, you know," she said, her eyes still on the orange horizon as the sun set.

He eased closer to her, drawing his knees up and resting his arms on them. "Jealous of what?"

"The women calling you. I'm sure that's why your phone vibrates and rings every half hour."

Stefan laughed. Victoria had never been one to mince words or back away from any uncomfortable topic. She was also very confident, like most American women were. He found that quality extremely sexy. What had that jerk Alex been thinking? Stefan only hoped they didn't run into the guy once they were back in L.A. Or if they did, he hoped the media wasn't around. The last thing he needed was a picture of him popping the other guy in his pretty-boy face.

"Go ahead and laugh," she went on. "But I know that's your entourage calling."

"And how do you know this?" He chuckled again, now at her description.

"Because if it had been your brother, one of your staff or anyone else important, you would've answered it."

He shook his head. "Possibly."

With a wide, sinful smile, she turned to face him. "So you admit your harem has been calling?"

"Maybe, but with the way you can't keep your hands off my body, I don't have time for others."

Victoria's laugh washed over him. "Your ego is even bigger than your bank accounts. I think we both know who initiated the sex this afternoon."

"You were the one who insisted on changing clothes. In a man's mind, that's code for 'I'm getting naked and you should join me.'"

"Oh, please." She rolled her eyes, still smiling. "If a woman says 'I'm going to the grocery store,' a man thinks that's a code for 'let's get naked.'"

Stefan didn't want to feel guilty about the women calling him. He couldn't help it. The fact he was married wasn't exactly a secret; it had been televised for the entire world to see. But a few of the women from his past knew him too well and had convinced themselves this marriage was a lie.

"Are you just a little jealous?" he asked, throwing her another smile.

Part of him wanted her to be, but the other part of him hoped she kept their relationship light and carefree.

Yes, he'd wanted Victoria on an intimate level for years, but now he had her where he wanted her. He didn't need emotions or anything too deep to creep into this new relationship they had discovered.

"I'm not jealous." She looked him dead in the eye, no smile, no glimmer of amusement. "But I won't be the other woman or played to look like a fool ever again."

Stefan turned, grabbed her by the shoulders and met her eyes. "There's no way in hell I'd ever treat you that way, Tori. And I'm not that jerk you were engaged to. Remember that."

He'd be damned if he'd let that bastard play the third wheel in their relationship, no matter their carefree set-up.

On a sigh, her head drooped. "I'm sorry. I don't have trust issues with you, Stefan. My mind just instantly ventured in the wrong direction."

"Hey." He placed a finger beneath her chin and lifted her face to meet his once again. "This marriage may not be a traditional one, but I say from here on out we keep your ex and my past out of it. Deal?"

"Deal."

The quick snapping of an automatic camera had him jerking his attention around.

He spotted a man crouched in the lush plants surrounding what was supposed to be the private beach to his family's palace.

Stefan jumped to his feet and took off after the unwanted intruder. "Stop," he yelled.

Hot sand squished beneath his feet, making him slide with each step. By the time he'd gotten to the area where the man had been in hiding, the guy was gone.

What the hell had the intruder overheard?

Stefan pulled his cell from his pocket and punched a button. "There's a man on the grounds," Stefan said before his security guard could utter a word. "If you find him first, take his camera. Then call the cops. I'm looking near the beach. Take the front of the palace."

Knowing Victoria would be fine for a few minutes, Stefan moved through the foliage in the direction the trespasser took off. No way in hell was he letting someone invade his privacy, and on his own secluded beach, as well.

Even though he knew without a doubt that Victoria didn't think anything of flashing bulbs and media circuses, he wanted their marriage, their life to be private. The bond they shared was so special, and even though the paparazzi had them practically married as teens, he didn't want their engagement or wedding tarnished. What transpired between him and Victoria was nobody's business.

But he had to find the guy and find out exactly what he'd overheard and take that damn camera. He couldn't afford for this secret to get out before the coronation. This country was his, damn it, and he'd do anything to keep it.

Besides, he wanted Tori all to himself…he was selfish like that. He wouldn't share her with the public any more than necessary.

More than anything, though, he wanted to shield her, protect her from any more pain. Because he cared for her more than any other woman in his life, he wanted to be the one to ride to her rescue and keep her life worry-free and happy.

Stefan spotted footprints in the sand and followed them up the embankment toward the tiny village. Sweat trickled down his back, but the heat was nothing compared to the anger in knowing someone had infiltrated his home. What the hell had his guards been doing? A discussion he'd be taking up later with the head of his security.

Stefan stopped when he spotted the man crouched down on the sidewalk, holding his camera, and from what Stefan could see, the man was looking through his shots. Probably checking to see if he needed to come back for more.

Without a sound, Stefan moved in from behind and wrapped an arm around the guy's neck, hauling him up to his feet.

"Drop the camera," Stefan growled in his ear.

Immediately the camera clattered to ground. With his free hand, Stefan pulled his cell from his pocket and dialed security to come collect the trash.

"You made a mistake in trespassing," Stefan told him, tightening his grip. "I don't take kindly to people invading my wife's privacy."

"I'm sorry," the man choked out. "Please."

"Whatever you *think* you overheard, forget it. If I even suspect you've gone to the media with lies, there won't be a place you can hide that I won't find you." Stefan loosened his hold but kept the guy in a lock until backup arrived. "I better never catch you on my property or even looking in my family's direction again or a smashed camera will be the least of your worries."

The heavy pounding of footsteps had Stefan shouting for the guards. "Over here," he yelled.

Once the guards had the trespasser secure, Stefan stepped around to get a good look at the man's face so he could remember it. Then he crouched down, picked up the broken camera and pulled the memory card out, sliding it into his pocket.

"Take him to the front while you wait for the cops," Stefan ordered his guards.

Tamping down his anger and wiping the sweat off his forehead, Stefan made his way back to Victoria. Her long, golden hair danced around in the ocean breeze, her face tilted up while she watched the water as if her privacy hadn't just been invaded.

"We secured the guy. Cops are on their way, and I personally confiscated the memory card." Stefan took a seat beside her. "Sorry about that."

With a shrug, Victoria turned to face him. "I'm used to it. Privacy really means nothing to me. I wouldn't know what to do with complete seclusion."

Stefan knew with her family she came into this world in the spotlight, but something about her statement struck him. She wasn't asking for privacy; no doubt she thought that was something she could never have. But why couldn't he provide her a little escape?

"What did he overhear?" she asked.

"I didn't give him the chance to say, but I made it very clear he's not to repeat anything or he will be found and dealt with."

Tori gasped. "You threatened him?"

"What did you want me to do? Ask him over for tea?"

On a sigh, Victoria shook her head. "I don't know. I just hope he didn't hear us. Pictures are one thing..."

Stefan wouldn't let some overeager cameraman ruin his future, or Victoria's. No matter the cost. He also wouldn't let the bastard ruin his day with his wife, either.

"Remember when we first met and we were trying to hide from all the cameras and crew for the film your mother was in?"

A genuine, beautiful smile spread across her face. "That was fun. We were purposely avoiding anybody so we could do whatever we wanted."

Stefan pictured the time in his mind, so clear and vivid. "I believe that's when I introduced you to alcohol."

On a groan, Victoria closed her eyes. "Don't remind me. I was so set on impressing you, I didn't want you to know I hadn't drank before."

"The look on your face after your first sip of whiskey kind of gave you away," he told her.

"You probably thought I was such a loser." She laughed, lying back on the blanket and looking up at the clear, blue sky.

"A loser? Nah. I thought you were innocent, and that's the kind of girl I was interested in."

And he had been…well, as much as a teenage boy could be interested in a girl. She'd been California fresh with all that silky blond hair and tanned skin. He'd instantly had a crush but had to play it cool.

So he did what any good boy would do. He'd plied her with alcohol and tried to talk her into skinny-dipping.

"You mean the kind of girl you were interested in corrupting?" she asked with a low laugh that made him pause to enjoy such sweetness.

There was just something about her that always made him smile. Their friendship never had any speed bumps, and for years he'd found himself wondering what something more with her would be like.

Of course, marriage to anyone never entered his mind, but so far being married to Tori really had its perks. She was playful in bed, and he appreciated the fact she wasn't getting too involved on a more heartfelt level.

"Maybe a little corrupting," he agreed. "I never did get you to go skinny-dipping."

Victoria shook her head. "That's something I've never done. It just sounds so…cold."

His eyes roamed over her body. She'd forgone the jeans and shirt and had ended up donning a beautiful pale blue strapless romper, and he wanted to slide his fingers between her breasts, loosen the knot and see the material puddle to the ground.

"Trust me." His eyes came back up to meet hers. "When I get you naked in the water, you'll be anything but cold."

Her breath hitched as she bit her lip and dropped her eyes to his mouth. Hell yeah. She was sexy personified, and she was all his for the next six months. After that... well, that ball was in her court. Going back to dating, and bedding, other women surprisingly wasn't a priority, not with Tori matching him both in bed and out.

Stefan slid one hand through her hair, his other hand cupping the side of her face. With the utmost care and tenderness, he tilted her head and secured his lips to hers. With gentle persuasion he coaxed her lips apart, pleased when she accommodated him. Her soft moan as she eased into his body aroused him more than all their frenzied kisses. Those fast-paced kisses were stepping stones to sex. This gentle, passionate kiss was a stepping stone to...what?

He told himself he was just enjoying the moment and not getting deeper intimately with her. Stefan didn't want to go down that path. But he did want to keep savoring his wife. He wanted to slowly strip her and see her body in the sunlight on the beach as he...

His cell phone chimed, breaking the moment. With a muttered curse, he eased back from those tender, swollen lips.

After jerking the phone from his pocket he answered, "Yes?"

"The police are here," the guard told him. "Would you like to come and talk to them or do you want me to take care of it?"

Stefan stared at Victoria. The moment of reminiscing had turned intense...something he hadn't counted on. Sex was one thing, but that flutter in his chest was not welcome.

Na pari i eychi. The woman was almost too perfect for

him. He couldn't afford to let himself get all emotional about their arrangement. He was a man—one known for his physical relationships. He had to remember that here.

"I'll be right there," he said before disconnecting the call.

Stefan came to his feet, put his hands on his hips and looked down at Victoria. "Police arrived. I'm going to go talk with them."

Still staring into his eyes, as if searching for answers about what had just happened, Victoria nodded and remained silent.

What *had* just happened? He didn't even know himself, but it was far too much. Besides, he couldn't focus on that right now.

"I can send someone to pick up our picnic later," he told her. "Are you staying here or coming back with me?"

"I think I'll stay here."

He studied her, trying to read if she was uncomfortable or just confused like he was. Was she feeling something beyond their friendship and sexual desire?

"Then I'll send someone down to make sure you're all right by yourself."

Victoria smiled. "I don't need a sitter, Stefan. I'll be fine. Go on and talk to the police. But you have the man's memory card, so don't be in a rush to press charges."

That was his Victoria. Always wanting the good in life to override the bad. She was a special woman and for now she was not just his best friend, she was his wife. He refused to delve deeper than that.

Victoria slid into her red silk nightgown and smoothed her hair back over her shoulder. The phone calls Stefan had been receiving shouldn't still be in the forefront of her mind, but they were, and she hated the fact she let the jealousy settle there for so long.

Stefan wasn't Alex. Stefan was the most loyal friend she'd ever had and no way would she compare the two men because Alex didn't even deserve the time of her thoughts.

What did deserve her thoughts were those blasted designs. Something just wasn't clicking. She'd never encountered this before, where all of the drawings weren't up to her own standards of perfection. Granted, they may be okay for some designers, but Victoria prided herself on flawless, shockingly stunning designs before she let anyone see them, and she wasn't going to change her ways with this new bridal collection.

She wanted her team back in L.A. to gasp with awe when they saw what she'd come up with. Unfortunately, if she took these current drawings to the table, her associates would only gasp in fright.

On the bright side, her random drawings of various forms of the Alexander family crest were quite impressive, if she did say so herself. Too bad that wasn't her main focus.

Soon-to-be brides around the world were waiting with high expectations to see what Victoria Alexander, Princess and almost Queen of Galini Isle, would come up with for the launching of her new line.

Maybe if she added a touch more lace. Lace said romance, but too much could scream tacky. Perhaps longer trains like so many girls dreamed of. Grown women still kept that little girl fairy tale in their mind. Their wedding day was supposed to be magical, and it all started with the dress because it set the tone.

Warm, strong hands cupped her shoulders and Victoria jumped.

"Easy."

She turned in Stefan's arms and smiled. "I didn't hear you come in."

His eyes dipped down to the V in her nightgown and a wicked grin spread across his lips. "Why cover up? Inside this room there should be a no-clothes rule."

Victoria rolled her eyes. "I barely get them on before you take them off."

"Exactly," he agreed, squeezing her almost-bare shoulders. "It's a waste of time. So tell me what had your mind so preoccupied?"

Reaching up, Victoria grabbed his forearms and held on. Sometimes it was just nice to have his strength, his shoulder to lean on. He never judged her and always listened with the compassion that only a best friend could.

"I've just hit a rough spot with the designs." Fear gripped her at the thought of being stuck in a rut, at the idea that she may be tapped out at the moment in her career she needed her creativity most. "This has never happened."

"You're stressing yourself," Stefan told her. "Take another day off to think about it. For that matter, take the rest of our time here off. Maybe once we get back to L.A., when you're in your element, the ideas will flow."

She hoped, but she couldn't count on what-ifs to get her through her career. Idly sitting by while waiting for something spectacular to jump in her mind wasn't how she worked. But taking a few days off couldn't hurt. It's not like the designs could get worse.

Offering a smile, she nodded. "You're right. I probably just need to get home."

Stefan slid her straps down her arms, the feather-soft touch of his fingertips she'd so quickly grown used to sending shivers all over her body. And her body never failed to respond to him since they'd first made love in the theater.

Made love? Yes, she felt confident using that phrase—

though she doubted Stefan would be. She loved him as her best friend, and the special relationship they had was unique. Granted this marriage may not be like many others, but at least they had a strong bond that was lacking in so many other couples.

"Now, since we have through the end of the week to enjoy this honeymoon phase," Stefan said, backing her toward the four-poster bed, "what do you say we continue making use of this alone time?"

And who could argue with a sexy Greek prince?

Seven

Stefan knew he wouldn't get out of Galini Isle without his entourage following him. While he was used to the guards being underfoot, now that he was king—or very soon to be—they took the role even more seriously.

Victoria didn't seem to mind the extras at her impressive Hollywood Hills home. Then again, her mind hadn't been on much else other than her designs. She'd drawn on the flight, she'd stayed up all hours of the night back in Greece, and she was still struggling.

Stefan hated to see her being so hard on herself. They'd been back in L.A. for only a few hours and she was already downtown at her office speaking with some of her staff.

The woman was a workaholic, but he admired her more than nearly anyone he knew. He also had a little surprise for her, hopefully to help get her creativity flowing in the direction she needed.

"Sir."

Stefan turned from the view of the city and faced the open living area to see his assistant, Hector, standing in the arched doorway.

"Yes?"

The man, who had been assistant to his father before his death, stepped forward.

"If you have a moment, Sir, we need to go over your schedule of events while we are in the States."

Stefan nodded. "Has something changed, Hector? I know Victoria and I are scheduled for the homeless shelter and a library appearance to help with funding."

"Yes, sir, but Her Highness's alma mater called and wanted to know if you both could put in an appearance. They were hoping to have a special dinner to honor the two of you. It won't be for a couple of weeks if you agree, because we'd need time to set up security."

Stefan sighed. "Let me ask her, but I don't think it will be a problem," he told Hector. "I can let you know by this evening. I don't want to disrupt her while she's at work."

Hector bowed. "Of course, sir. I will check for a spot on the schedule that will accommodate both of you should she agree."

When Hector quieted but remained standing and staring, Stefan smiled. "Is there something else?"

Hector's lips barely lifted into a grin, but he merely nodded. "You know I don't like to put my nose into anyone's business, but—"

Stefan chuckled. "It's your job to do so, yet you apologize for it every time you interfere. There's always a valid reason, so let's hear what it is."

Stefan gestured to the wraparound sofa and took a seat. "Something is on your mind because you've waited until Victoria left to come to me."

The elderly man sat, not fully relaxing because he remained on the edge of the cushions. "With Victoria gone, perhaps this would be a perfect time to call one of her brothers."

Stefan shrugged. "I will. But, I'd like to see them in person. They don't normally do documentaries, so I need to present all the facts before they can make a decision."

"Have you told Victoria about your idea yet?" Hector asked.

Shaking his head, Stefan replied, "No. She's so busy with work, and this really doesn't involve her."

Hector came to his feet. "Everything in your life now involves her. I wouldn't keep this to yourself too much longer, Your Majesty."

As was custom, Hector bowed before leaving the room.

His loyal assistant was under the illusion the marriage with Victoria was genuine, so of course he thought this idea involved her. Stefan would tell Victoria if her brothers agreed to the film. But right now she was busy and she'd already done so much by taking on this marriage and title. He wasn't going to pile more on her plate. He had to speak to Bronson and Anthony first, and he didn't want Victoria to feel as if she were obligated to help or caught in the middle.

Would they even go for something like this? Stefan didn't know Anthony very well, but he knew Bronson well enough to ask if he would entertain the idea.

A documentary with the Dane and Price names behind it would no doubt kill any suspicion that the film wasn't thoroughly researched and executed. That reputation of the filmmakers would certainly carry a lot of clout in clearing up the speculation of his father's involvement in his mother's untimely death.

Just because his father had admitted an extramarital affair, that didn't mean he'd planned an accident to remove his own wife from the picture so he could be with his mistress. Nor did it mean his mother had taken her own life. The curvy roads were slick, the brakes needed changing—a fact that had come out later from the police report—and his mother had insisted on not using a driver that day. The series of events led up to a tragedy, but Stefan refused to blame his father.

Oh, he'd blamed him at the time. Yelled and cursed at him for not loving his mother enough and for going around having an affair, but once Stefan saw the grief, the anguish that his father had gone through, even up to his own death, Stefan realized that his father was only human. His father may have strayed from the marriage once, but the man had been completely in love with his wife.

Stefan came to his feet again and moved to the floor-to-ceiling window, where he admired a view of the city in the distance. Somewhere in the crazy overpopulated town was his wife, his best friend. He wanted her opinion, but she had so much on her plate already and he hated to bother her with his own issues. Wasn't she already going above and beyond by helping him secure the crown and keep his country independent? He didn't want to make her feel like she needed to step in and persuade her brothers to agree to the film. Besides, as of this point, taking the blemish off his father's reputation didn't concern her.

Right now he wanted her to concentrate on her designs, on letting her creativity flow and her natural spirit shine through. She'd already done enough for him, and he wasn't going to ask for another favor for a really long time…unless he asked her to don a certain type of lingerie, and that didn't count as a favor when the enjoyment was mutual.

Raking a hand through his hair, Stefan recalled that Victoria's mother was planning a dinner party tomorrow. If the right time presented itself, he'd approach Bronson, but this wasn't something he'd announce at the table. He really did want to keep this quiet until he knew for sure this was a project Bronson and Anthony were willing to take on.

As the next king of Galini Isle, Stefan felt it was not only his duty as the son of a man wrongfully accused, but he also knew telling the truth was the right thing to do to keep his family's name and honor one of integrity.

And he hoped like hell that intruder on his property had taken the threat seriously, otherwise he'd have a whole new mess on his hands. He already had enough to deal with without worrying if his country was secure. So far this marriage was getting him closer and closer to his title. He couldn't lose it now.

As he glanced around the spacious, brightly decorated living room, he couldn't help but wonder what would happen at the end of the six-month period. Would Victoria stay with him? He had to admit, being married to his best friend was much better than he ever would've dreamed. And once they put in a few royal appearances now that their honeymoon phase was over and they were in L.A., Tori would get an even better sampling of what being royalty truly meant. Perhaps she wouldn't like all the hype and responsibilities.

He moved to a built-in bookcase and gazed over the snapshots of Victoria with her family and friends through the years. There were even a couple shots of the two of them together. In one they were laughing, Victoria's hand on his chest. The captured scene ran through his mind and he recalled that day so vividly. He'd come to visit her—it was actually one of the times he'd been about to tell her he wanted to explore a physical relationship. They'd been at a restaurant opening for a mega-movie star who had started a chain, and the media was swarming, waiting to get pictures of all the rich and famous.

He'd pulled her aside and asked her if they could skip the event. When she'd told him it was rude, he told him he'd rather be having a root canal without painkiller and she'd started laughing. Someone in the press had snapped the picture, and it had ended up in several media outlets with speculation that the two of them were more than friends.

But now fate had handed him this opportunity, and he didn't intend to screw it up. While he may not have married Victoria for love, he did respect her, and she was a perfect match for him. After all, she'd grown up in the spotlight as well, and they knew going in that their privacy was limited.

Besides, Victoria had her own life goals and issues to keep her occupied. Which was why he'd keep this documentary idea to himself until he found out if anything more would come of it.

He hoped the opportunity would arise tomorrow night to discuss possibilities with Bronson so he could finally bury his parents in his heart with the respect they both deserved.

Frustrated didn't even come close to describing the emotions swirling inside her.

Victoria let herself into her Hollywood Hills home and smiled at Stefan's permanent bodyguard/assistant positioned by the door. That would take some getting used to, but she was technically on her way to being a queen, so just one more thing she'd have to deal with…eventually. Right now she'd put it on the back burner because she didn't have the time or the energy to even think about her royal crown or any of the duties expected of her.

Her wedding gown designs were improving but still not to the point where she was ready to start whipping out her needle and thread.

Her team had bounced around ideas all day, and by the time four o'clock rolled around, Victoria was ready to strangle herself with a bolt of satin.

She bypassed the living area and headed straight up the wide, curved marble staircase that led to the second-story bedrooms. She assumed Stefan was around somewhere because his guard was at his post.

When she went into her walk-in closet, she slid off her Ferragamo pumps and sank her toes into the plush carpet. After unzipping her sheath dress, she folded it onto the shelf, where she had a pile that needed to go to the cleaners. Obviously something she'd forgotten to have done before her whirlwind proposal, marriage and step up the royal ladder.

Did royalty even worry about such mundane things as dry cleaning? Of course, people may think a member of the prestigious Dane family didn't, either.

Bracing her hands on the shoe island in her closet, Victoria bowed her head and sighed. She'd never felt out of control, never felt so overwhelmed that she wanted to burst into tears, but she was definitely there now.

How had her life become so out of control? How had all of her decisions, goals and dreams slipped away and turned into something else she didn't even recognize? She'd never had a problem designing before. But now that she was married and struggling with her rapidly growing emotions, she just couldn't concentrate.

Between work and Stefan, she was a mess of jumbled-up nerves.

Tears pricked her eyes, her throat burned and she shook her head. No. Tears solved nothing and feeling sorry for herself wouldn't help put life back on track where she was comfortable.

"Well, this is nice to see." Stefan entered the closet,

eyes roaming over her matching lace bra and panty set she was left standing in. But when his gaze landed back on her face, all joking and sexual looks vanished. "What's wrong? Are you okay?"

He closed the gap between them, taking her in his arms and holding her against his chest. And wasn't that just like him? Always ready to comfort, always ready to rescue the distressed damsel?

Victoria sniffed. "I'm just being overly dramatic today. Chalk it up to being female."

"Well, honey, you've been female the whole time I've known you, and it takes a lot to bring a strong woman like you to tears." He eased back, swiped at her damp cheeks and stared into her eyes with the compassion she'd always known from him. "Want to talk about it? Is it work?"

She had to be honest. He was her husband, after all, so they should share everything. And in some ways he knew her better than she knew herself, so he would most likely know if she was holding something back.

"I think everything just hit me," she told him. "Work, marriage. It's all moving so fast, I don't feel like I'm in control anymore."

He kissed her forehead. "You're in control, Tori. You just always put this pressure on yourself to excel and be the best, which is great, but sometimes you need to give yourself a break."

She studied his face, that handsome face that so many women dreamed about, and smiled. "Is that what you would do? Take a break?"

He shrugged. "Probably not, but I don't like to see you upset."

"You don't get upset?"

"Upset? No. I do get angry, which fuels me to work harder."

Her smile spread wider and she tilted her head.

"I get it," he said, laughing. "Those were angry tears?"

"Frustrated tears," she corrected. "But at this point, same thing."

He leaned forward, kissed her gently and stepped back. "Why don't you throw on some clothes and meet me downstairs."

Comfortable with her body, Victoria placed her hands on her hips. "Now I know the honeymoon's over." She laughed. "I'm standing here nearly naked and you're telling me to throw on clothes."

Heat instantly filled his eyes as he raked his gaze over her. "Oh, believe me, I'm having a very hard time being noble here, but sex isn't what you need right now. Just get dressed and come downstairs. Or wear that, but my guard will see more of you than I'm willing to share."

Stefan turned and left, leaving her staring after him.

Some married women didn't have a tenth of the connection she had with Stefan. And even though they married under less than traditional circumstances, she knew she had a good thing going…if she could just keep her emotions in check.

She threw on a pair of white shorts and a flowy green top. After sliding into a pair of gold sandals, she made her way downstairs. She didn't see the guard by the door, but she knew he wasn't far. Thankfully he did try to stay out of sight and give them privacy.

Victoria saw Stefan through the patio doors. She crossed the living room and walked out the open set of French doors to the warmth of the evening SoCal sunshine.

Stefan sat on one of the plush outdoor sofas she'd recently added and Victoria took a seat next to him.

"What's that?" She pointed to the small folder he held

on his lap. "Did you draw some secret, magical designs you're willing to share with me?"

He laid the folder on her legs. "Open it."

Intrigued, she pulled back the cover flap and gasped. "Stefan…" Page after page, she shuffled through designs and even some of the crazy doodling she'd done as a teen. "Where did you get these?"

"I kept them."

She eyed the papers, yellowing around the edges, and looked at him. "But…why?"

With a shrug, he turned to face her. "When you came to visit, you were always doodling and talking about being a designer. Sometimes I'd keep the papers you left laying around. I knew you'd make a name for yourself because you've always been so determined. You had such *pathos,* a passion, for designing." He laughed. "Even then you would sketch random images to help you think clearer."

Emotions clogged her throat and, dammit, for the second time today she was going to cry. Even all those years ago he'd had faith in her.

"These are, well…terrible." She laughed through watery tears.

He put a hand over hers, taking his other hand to cup her chin and hold his gaze. "They may be terrible to you, but they were your dream, Victoria. Look at them. Look close. You may see something ugly, but I see a promise that a young girl made to herself."

Oh, God. How did the man always know what to say?

"You're right," she whispered. "I just can't believe you kept them."

His hand dropped from her face. "Maybe I wanted to keep them so that when you became famous I could sell them."

A laugh burst from her. "You're so rich, you never would've thought to sell these."

His eyes settled on hers, and the heat she saw staring back at her had the smile dying on her lips.

"Maybe I saw the talent," he told her. "Maybe the crush I had on you prompted me to keep them."

Victoria's heart clenched. "Stefan, you didn't have feelings for me then."

"I did," he confessed. "I may have been young and foolish, but I did care more for you then than any other girl I knew."

Victoria couldn't handle this. Couldn't think what that revelation could've meant for the course of their relationship had he told her his feelings at the time.

"I'd hate to think if we dated seriously as teens or in our twenties we would've lost each other as friends. Besides that, you would've disappointed all those ladies," she joked. "Good thing you grew out of it, huh?"

Something she didn't recognize, or didn't want to recognize, flitted through his eyes. "Yeah, good thing."

As Victoria looked down at her designs, she remembered dreaming as she'd been drawing them. Dreaming of her wedding day, of her groom waiting at the end of the aisle.

And in all her dreaming, that man had been a prince. A prince who knew her inside and out, who cared for her as a friend and lover, who would do anything to make her happy.

Victoria could no longer deny that she was teetering on the edge of falling in love with her husband, and that out-of-control emotion scared her to death.

Eight

Stefan sat back and watched the chaos—otherwise known as dinner with his in-laws—which was becoming a little too hearth and homey to him between the newlyweds and the babies.

Bronson and his wife, Mia, took turns holding and feeding their little Bella, whom he believed Victoria told him was almost a year old now.

Victoria's other brother, Anthony, was holding histwo-month-old baby girl as Charlotte fed the eighteen-month-old Lily in her high chair.

And through all the cries, spit-ups and diaper changes, the Grand Dane of Hollywood, Olivia Dane, sat at the head of the long, elegantly accessorized table and smiled. Either the woman didn't realize that in a year or so her immaculate Beverly Hills home would be a giant playground or she was so in love with her family she didn't care that her fine china could end up in millions of shards on her marble floor.

"Bella, no, honey."

Stefan glanced to the other end of the table where Bella was throwing some orange, liquid concoction onto the floor. Why did all baby food look like already recycled dinner in a jar?

"Oh, don't worry about it." Olivia waved a hand. "Marie can clean it up when she clears the table later."

"No, I'll get it." Mia came to her feet and whipped out a bunch of wipes from who knows where. Obviously moms had a knack for always being ready for anything.

"I think Carly needs a diaper change," Charlotte said as she came to her feet, holding her baby to her chest. "I'll be right back."

Anthony stood, taking the infant. "Let me. Go ahead and finish eating."

Victoria laughed. "I love seeing my big strong brothers taking care of baby poop and puke."

Stefan dropped his fork to his plate with a clatter. "And that's the end of my dinner."

Patting his leg, Victoria laughed. "Oh, toughen up, Prince. Your day will come."

A shudder coursed through him at the thought of children being written into the archaic laws of his land. To be honest, he was surprised they weren't, but at the same time he was thankful.

And just as quickly as that shudder spread through him, another took over as he glanced to Victoria's smiling face. An image of her swollen with his child did something unrecognizable to his belly, his heart. He didn't want to examine the unwanted emotions any further because if she were ever swollen with a baby, it more than likely wouldn't be his.

She was on birth control. Besides, they hadn't even discussed kids. They hadn't discussed beyond the six months, other than to joke, much less anything permanent or long term.

"You okay?" Victoria asked in a low whisper. "You're staring with a weird look on your face."

He shook off the thoughts and returned her warm smile. "Fine. I admit I'm not used to babies, so all of this is new to me."

"We weren't, either," she admitted, placing her cloth napkin onto the table. "But we adjusted quickly, and I couldn't imagine our lives without all these little cuties."

He studied her face once again, wondering if she did indeed have babies in her dream for life. Had he put that aspiration on hold when he'd selfishly asked her to be his wife? Hell, he hadn't even asked, he'd basically begged…a moment he wasn't very proud of, but nonetheless he'd had no choice. Once she'd mentioned wanting a family someday, but was that still a desire? And if so, where would that leave them and their marriage?

Discussing her fantasies of a family would have to wait. For one thing he didn't think the topic was appropriate conversation at the dinner table with her family, and he had to speak with Anthony or Bronson, hopefully both, about his documentary idea.

Unfortunately, the right time had not presented itself.

Olivia scooted her chair back, the heavy wood sliding over the dark marble floor. "If everyone is done eating, we can go into the living room where the kids can play on the floor."

Stefan came to his feet and pulled Victoria's chair out for her.

"You married a prince and he pulls out your chair," Mia said, then turned to Bronson. "Are you taking notes?"

Bronson laughed, and glanced at Stefan. "Give a guy a break, would ya? You're making me look bad."

Victoria wrapped an arm around Stefan's waist and squeezed. "Can't help it if my man is always a gentleman, Bron. Looks like you need to step up your game."

Stefan didn't miss the way Bronson studied how Victoria was holding on to him, and he didn't miss the way the look of surprise resonated when Victoria said "my man."

Just where were they headed? And why the hell was it important for him to know? He was a man for crying out loud. The sex was amazing, she wasn't demanding of his time and she hadn't asked him for anything. Why was he suddenly analyzing everything like a damn woman?

Anthony came back in as they were all moving from the room. "She's all ready to go," he announced, handing Carly back to Charlotte.

Olivia went to get Lily from her high chair when Bronson spoke up.

"You ladies go on ahead," he said. "I'd like to talk with Anthony and Stefan."

Okay, so now the moment of opportunity had presented itself, but Stefan had a feeling this wasn't going to be the time to bring up his favor, not with the look Bronson was giving him.

Because he tended to be spiteful, Stefan leaned down and gave Victoria a kiss—and not a simple see-ya-later peck.

What he and Victoria decided to do with their marriage was nobody else's business, and he would fight for their privacy no matter who he went up against.

"Fine with me," Olivia said. "I'm just glad you're all not talking about the film."

"We just haven't gotten to it, yet," Anthony piped up.

"We will. Don't worry. We're only a few months into the shoot, still plenty to discuss."

"Yes, I'm aware of the time frame." Olivia rolled her eyes and adjusted a wiggly Lily in her arms. "I should've known better than to think we'd get through the night without shop talk."

"Play nice with the other boys," Victoria said with a wink.

Obviously she missed the way Bronson was throwing daggers. "Always," Stefan promised.

Once the ladies and babies were gone, Bronson crossed his arms over his chest. "What the hell kind of game are you playing with my sister?"

"No game." Relaxed, Stefan rested a hand on the back of his chair. "And before you get all big brother on me, let me tell you that I will not share how Victoria and I treat this marriage. It's none of your concern."

Anthony cleared his throat. "Excuse me, but did I miss something in the two minutes it took to change a diaper?"

"Stefan seemed to be on more than friendly terms with Victoria," Bronson supplied. "I'm just trying to make sure he's not playing a game with her. She's been hurt before."

"Bronson." Anthony sighed. "Simmer down. Stefan and Victoria are grown adults. If they want to…whatever, then that's their business."

Bronson cursed. "Did either of you pay attention when that jerk broke her heart? Did you hear her crying? See the way her self-esteem lowered? I won't watch someone I love go through that again."

Guilt tore at Stefan that Victoria had gone through all of that and he hadn't been able to help her more. But with his father's illness and death, there was just no way to be in two places at once.

Just the thought of her crying over some jerk who wasn't

worth her tears made his gut clench. She deserved all the happiness and love life could give.

"Listen," Stefan said. "We know what we're doing. Yes, we've grown closer than just friends, but that's our business. I won't explain our actions to you or anyone else."

Anthony chuckled. "Guess that settles that discussion."

Refusing to back down, Stefan continued to stare at Bronson. No, he hadn't heard the cries from Victoria because she'd always been so strong on the phone, but he knew she'd been hurt. A woman like Victoria who loved with her whole heart and was loyal to a fault couldn't come out of a relationship like that and not be scarred.

And he was no better than Alex. Wasn't he using her as well to gain a title? The only difference was he'd told her up front.

"I won't let her get hurt again," Bronson said. "I hate to sound all big and bad, but I had to tell you where I stand."

Stefan nodded. "Duly noted."

"If you two are done kissing and making up, can we get back to our family night?" Anthony asked.

Stefan knew an opening when he saw one. "Actually, I'd like to run something by you two since I have you here together."

Bronson gestured toward the doors. "Let's go out on the patio then."

Bronson led the way out the glass double doors and onto the stone patio surrounded by lush plants and flowers and a trickling waterfall.

Stefan took a seat in one of the iron chairs and waited for Victoria's brothers to get comfortable on the outdoor sofa across from him.

"What's up?" Bronson asked.

"I know you're both aware that my mother passed away when I was younger and there was speculation that she either committed suicide or my father may have had something to do with the accident."

When both men nodded, Stefan went on. "I have wanted to clear my family's name because my father never would go public before. He just wanted the rumors to die down, and he feared if he kept bringing it up people would assume he was covering his own tracks. Well, now that he's gone, I want to shed some light on the situation and prove that he had nothing to do with her accident, nor did she, and they did indeed love each other very much."

Anthony eased forward in his seat. "What do you have in mind?"

"I know that you two don't normally take on projects like this, but I was hoping we could discuss working on a documentary." Stefan wanted to hold his breath and wait for a response, but at the same time, he wanted to keep talking to convince them. "I have proof my father had nothing to do with the accident and that my mother wasn't depressed or suicidal. There's not a doubt in my mind that while, yes, he had an affair, he was not trying to get rid of my mother. The affair had been years before the accident, and when she died, I saw him go through pure hell. I just want to clear his reputation and go into my title with a clean slate for the Alexander name."

"You sound certain that this was an accident," Bronson said. "I'd be willing to discuss this further. I may not typically do documentaries, but that doesn't mean I'm not open to the possibility."

"I agree," Anthony said. "Could we set up a time to talk about this in greater detail? I mean, we'd have to look at the police reports and interview credible witnesses who are willing to come forward."

"I can provide you with anything you need." A spear of relief spread through Stefan. "Victoria and I are going to be here for another few months, so whenever you two are free, let me know. We have a few engagements coming up, but our schedule in the States is still pretty light. I can work around your shooting times."

As Victoria's brothers discussed their upcoming schedules, Stefan couldn't help but be overly thrilled. He had no idea they would be so open to the idea and respond so quickly. Though they hadn't agreed to anything, they hadn't shot down the idea.

Moving forward with this project and his coronation, Stefan knew that if everything fell in the right place, his life would be just as he'd pictured it. Clean family reputation and his country secured in the Alexander name.

What more could he want?

Nine

"So what did my brothers talk to you about?"

Victoria's fingertip circled the top of her wineglass as she eased forward in her seat. Stefan had taken her to her office, then afterward she wanted to show him a new restaurant that had opened. They were just having drinks and a dessert, but sometimes it was nice to get out of the house and enjoy society like a normal person—or as normal as one could be between her iconic family and her royal status.

With the outdoor seating and sunset in the distance, the ambiance screamed romance...even if a bodyguard was seated a few tables away trying to blend in.

Yeah, this was now her "normal" life.

Stefan shrugged. "Nothing much."

Victoria glared at him across the intimate table. "You're lying."

His eyes came up to meet hers as he reached across and

took her hand from her glass. He kissed her fingertips one at a time, and she relished the familiar shivers that crept over her body at his simple, yet passionate actions. But she wasn't letting the question go.

"Stefan?"

Lacing his hand through hers, he smiled. "Yes?"

"You've never been a good liar, and all this charm isn't working on me."

He quirked a dark brow. "Oh, yeah? I guarantee your heart rate is up, and I know you want to kiss me because you're watching my lips."

Busted.

"I'm watching your lips because I'm waiting for the truth to emerge from them." No way would she admit that he could do so little and turn her on. "Did Bronson get too protective?"

"We simply had a misunderstanding, and now we don't," Stefan said. "Men don't stay upset like women. He just wanted to discuss something, and it's over."

Victoria would make a special trip to Bronson's house. No way was she going to be sheltered or coddled by her brother.

"What was Anthony there for? Peacemaker?"

Stefan smiled. "He is quite a bit more laid back, yes?"

"He wasn't when Charlotte left him," Victoria replied. "I'd never seen a man so relentless on keeping his family together. He would've walked through hell for her."

"I'd do the same for you."

Victoria jerked at his automatic, non-hesitant response. Surely he wasn't developing feelings for her...not like she had for him. God, if he ever found out she'd fallen in love with him their friendship would be strained. Right now, with the playful sex and always hanging out, they had a good thing. No way would she put this relationship in jeopardy by revealing her true feelings.

"Stefan…"

"I realize their marriage is quite different from ours," he told her, stroking the back of her hand with his thumb. "But you're the one woman in my life that I would sacrifice anything for."

This was the point in a conversation where some women would think this was a major confession of love…Victoria was not one of those women. She knew Stefan better than any other woman did. He was a charmer, a playboy, but most of all, he did love her. In the way all best friends love each other.

But the romantic in her, the smidgen of a sparkle that hadn't been diminished by Alex, sighed and smiled internally at the idea that her husband would sacrifice anything for her.

"I'm ready to head home," he said, giving her a look that she knew had nothing to do with friendship and everything to do with lust. "Why don't you finish that drink."

"Forget the drink," she told him with a slight grin. "I have wine at home."

She grabbed her bag off the back of the iron chair and stood at the same time he was there to help her from her seat. When she turned, their lips were a breath apart and Stefan sealed them together briefly but firmly, loaded with promise.

"We need to leave before I really give the media something to print," he murmured against her mouth.

She swayed slightly and his warm, strong hand came around and settled firmly against her bare back where her summer dress dipped low. The heat from his touch did nothing to help her wave of dizziness brought on by pure desire.

She'd never had even a fraction of this passion with Alex. Mercy, she was in trouble.

"I've got you, Victoria. Always."

The heat in his eyes made her wish this were more than a marriage of convenience or a businesslike arrangement. But she was too afraid to explore that deeper level of emotion until she could see just where they stood at the end of the six months.

With a smile, she nodded. "I'm ready."

He led her from the cozy outdoor restaurant to the car that was waiting for them at the curb. Victoria's driver had been replaced with one of Stefan's guards, and the man instantly appeared, opened the door and let them into the backseat. As she slid across, her dress rode up high on her thigh. Stefan came in beside her and placed a hand over hers before she could pull the material down.

"Leave it," he said, hitting the button to put up the soundproof one-way window divider. "I have the best idea."

Oh, Lord.

As the guard brought the engine to life and pulled from the curb, Stefan turned on the intercom to tell the man to take his time heading back to Hollywood Hills.

An hour in the backseat of the limo with a man as seductive and sensual as Stefan? Victoria's body hummed and tightened in anticipation.

When he clicked the button off, he turned, sliding his other hand up her thigh and pushing both sides of the dress to her hips.

"Convenient you wore a dress," he murmured, staring down at her bare legs and the peek of yellow satin panties that were exposed. "Hate to waste this opportunity."

As his hands squeezed her thighs, his lips captured hers. The wine they'd drank tasted so good on his tongue, intoxicating her to the point she didn't care they were in the back of her car getting ready to have what she hoped was hot, wild sex.

When her hands came up around his neck, he eased back.

"Scoot down in the seat," he whispered. "I want this to be all about you."

And there was no woman in her right mind who would turn down an invitation like that.

Victoria did as he asked as he eased her legs farther apart. In his strong grasp, she felt the tug on her panties until she heard the material give way and tear.

"You owe me a pair of panties," she joked.

As he settled onto the floor between her legs, he gazed up at her beneath heavy lids. Bright eyes pierced hers as he said, "I prefer you without them."

With his wide shoulders holding her thighs apart, Victoria wondered if they were really doing this. Were they actually going to get intimate in the back of a car? And not only that, but this was far more personal than sex. Was Stefan taking their relationship to the next level? Obviously yes, but was he even aware of how personal this act was?

She didn't care and couldn't think anymore the second his finger slid over her, parting her a second before his mouth fixed on her.

Instinct had her sliding down even more. The way he made love to her with his mouth had her gripping his shoulders, the edge of the seat, the door handle, anything to keep from screaming at the overwhelming sensations rocketing through her.

In no time, her body quivered, bursts of pure bliss shooting through her. Stefan stayed with her until the last of her tremors ceased.

Reality hit her as he literally crawled back up her body.

Those talented hands slid over her curves, and he took a seat next to her, lifting her up to settle on his lap. As he nestled her into the crook of his arm, she tucked her face against his warm neck.

"You're not seriously going to try to hide the fact you're completely turned on, are you?" she asked.

His soft chuckle vibrated against his hard chest. "Kind of hard to hide it, but I wanted this to be about you. We can continue at home if you'd like."

Victoria lifted her head, wondering if Stefan realized how this moment, even though it was in the back of a car, had changed the course of their relationship. Did he get this intimate with all of his women? She closed her eyes briefly, trying to block out the instant mental images. If she had anything to say about it, he'd not be with any other woman ever again. He'd put the ball in her court at the end of the six months, and she was seriously considering staying, making him see just how this marriage could and should work for all the right reasons—which had absolutely nothing to do with his title.

But if she stayed, could she be a loyal, devoted queen and still design? She couldn't give up her own goals to cater to his, but she wanted this marriage to work. There had to be a way.

Stefan stared down at Victoria. Holy hell. What had just happened? He'd meant to be giving, passionate, but something changed…something he couldn't put his finger on. The way she looked at him with her face flushed and her lids heavy made him want to rip off both their clothes and satisfy her once again before finally relieving himself of this constant state of arousal he seemed to have around her lately.

"I want to make you happy, Stefan," she told him, stroking her fingertip down his cheek and along his jawline.

Yeah, something definitely changed. She wasn't smiling, wasn't playful. Her words, her actions were from the heart.

Was she sinking more into this marriage than she should? Granted, he'd always wondered how they'd be together, but if she was falling for him, could he ever give her that deeper, loving, marital bond in return? He honestly didn't think he had it in him.

God, he didn't want to hurt her. Right now all he wanted was to enjoy the way they were living together. Why couldn't that be enough?

"You've made me happy by helping me, Victoria."

"You know I could never tell you no," she replied, flashing him a sexy grin. "Besides, I'm getting what I want, too."

Friends and business. That's what this had to be…no matter what flutter he thought he felt in his chest earlier. The emotion had to be ignored. Victoria was too important to him to risk their bond on something as questionable as love.

As the driver wound his way up the Hollywood Hills, Victoria sat nestled against his side. He loved the familiar lavender scent that always surrounded her and the sexy way she would sigh as she crossed her legs and curved her body more into his. And now that he knew she wore nothing beneath that dress, well, *sexy* was a vast understatement.

He would let her show him her appreciation when they returned home. For now he needed to come to grips with the fact that he didn't want to get too involved in this marriage on a foundation he couldn't control, but when he'd taken their lovemaking to another level only moments ago, he'd done just that.

And he had no one to blame but himself.

Ten

Victoria's smile never faltered, and they'd been serving meals to homeless veterans for the past two hours. Her beauty radiated throughout the entire gymnasium of the old school where the Vets chatted and tried to capture a piece of her time,

He didn't blame them. Victoria was so easy to talk to, so easy to be around—the crowd would've never known that minutes before they'd come in she was nervous about fulfilling her first royal duty. He'd told her to be herself because she was a natural.

As she put the group at ease with her thankfulness for their services and the occasional gentle hug, Stefan continued to refill plates and cups. He let her use her charm on the room, and all the while the cameras were eating this up and proving to the world that she was the perfect woman for this position.

"Sir." Hector came up behind him and whispered, "The

cameraman would like you to stay closer to Victoria so he can capture your charity work together. That was the point of the visit."

Stefan glanced around the room of men and women who had given their all for their country…something Stefan could relate to. Guilt weighed heavily on his shoulders.

"I'm not here for a photo op, Hector." Stefan turned to face his assistant and lowered his voice. "I'm here to assist these people and show them that my wife and I care about them. I don't give a damn about the photographer. If he wants a good shot and story, tell him to take pictures of all these people who have been forgotten."

Hector folded his hands in front of him. "Sir, the whole reason for coming was to showcase your role as your country's leader and so the world could see you and Victoria as a united front."

Stefan sighed. "We are a united front, Hector. Tell the photographer he can nab a picture of us when we're done. We'll pose for one then. Until that point, we are here to help, not for some show for the world so they just *think* we are helping."

Hector nodded with a slight bow and walked off. When Stefan turned back with the pitcher of tea, an elderly man wearing a navy hat with his ship's name embroidered across the top was looking at him with tears in his eyes.

"Thank you," the man said.

Stefan looked down at the elderly man, who had scarred hands and a weathered face. "Nothing to thank me for, sir. I'm the one who needs to thank you."

The man used the edge of the table and the back of his chair to come to his feet. Stefan stepped back to give him room.

"I've never met royalty before, sir," the man said. "It is an honor to have you and your beautiful wife here. And for you two to be so caring…well, it just touches an old guy like me to know there are still people who give a damn."

Stefan held out his hand, waited for the man to shake it. "What's your name?"

"Lieutenant Raymond Waits," he replied, straightening his shoulders.

"I will personally see to it that this shelter is funded for as long as possible." Stefan would make it happen no matter what. "I will also make sure my wife and I schedule a stop here twice a year when we are in the States."

The handshake quickly turned to an embrace as Raymond put his free arm around Stefan. He hadn't meant to get on a soapbox, but dammit, he understood loyalty to a country, and these vets deserved respect and love.

"Now, I better get back to refilling drinks or you'll be my only friend here," Stefan said when the vet pulled back, trying to look away as if embarrassed by the tears in his eyes.

Raymond nodded, taking his seat. As Stefan moved on, he glanced up to see Victoria watching him from across the room, and he didn't miss the moisture that had gathered in her own eyes. Obviously she'd seen the emotional moment.

Stefan smiled and winked at her, trying to lighten the mood because the last thing he wanted was for her to believe he was some sort of hero. He was just doing what was right.

By the time they needed to leave to get across town to the library for a fund-raiser, Stefan had already discussed the funding with Hector, who was putting a plan into motion. Now this is what being powerful was all about. Why have such control if you couldn't use it for the greater good?

They posed for just a few pictures with some of the soldiers and promised to return. Stefan hated that a piece of his heart was left with this group of remarkable men and women. He wanted to rule his country while keeping his emotions in check, not tear up when he came across charity cases.

Victoria swiped tears away as they headed to their waiting car. Once settled inside, he pulled her against his side and sighed.

"You okay?" he asked.

"You're amazing." She sniffed. "I don't care if the media portrays you as a bad boy, Stefan. I know the truth, and you've just revealed it to a room full of thankful vets."

He didn't want to be commended for doing what was right and good. "I wish I could do more," he said honestly. "But we'll do what we can where we can."

Tori reached up, cupping his cheek, and shifted to face him. "You're one amazing king, Stefan."

She touched her lips to his, briefly, tenderly. But he didn't want gentle, he wanted hard, fast. Now. He wanted to feel her beneath him, feel her come undone around him.

His hand slid up her bare thigh and her breath caught.

"Didn't we just do this the other day?" she asked, smiling against his mouth.

"Glad I could make an impression," he murmured. "But I plan on torturing you until we get to the library. It is across town, you know. I may even continue for the ride home afterward."

She slid a hand up over his denim-clad leg and cupped him. "Torture can be a two-way street, you know."

"I'm counting on it."

As his mouth captured hers again, his hand snaked up beneath her dress. When his fingertip traveled along the edge of her lacy panties, her legs parted. Yeah, he wanted what she was offering, but foreplay was so much fun, and he wanted to relish these next few moments of driving her wild. He'd always considered himself a giving lover, but with Victoria he wanted to focus on her and her pleasure. Everything about touching her, kissing her was so much more arousing than seeking a fast release.

Her palm slid up and down over the zipper of his jeans…a zipper that was becoming increasingly painful.

He tore his lips from hers. "Tori, you're way too good at this game."

When she put both hands on his shoulders and slid to the floor between his legs, he swallowed hard. "Way too good," he repeated.

And thankfully he'd put the divider up between them and the driver because she was reciprocating the favor he'd given her a few days ago.

How was he ever going to get over all of this if she chose to leave?

Victoria couldn't stop smiling. Finally, she'd managed to take control, shut Stefan up and make him lose his mind all at once. Yeah, she was pretty proud of herself.

The ride to the library and then home was quite memorable…for both of them.

As they walked up the brick steps toward her front door, a car pulling into the circular drive had her turning back to see who the visitor was.

Her heart stopped, her body tensing at the unwelcome guest.

No. This couldn't be happening. What was he doing here?

"Victoria?" Stefan touched her arm. "Who is it?"

Before she could answer, the car came to a stop and Alex unfolded himself from the two-door red sports car.

"I'll talk to him," Stefan told her, jaw clenching. "You can go inside."

Victoria held up a hand and shook her head. "No, you go on in."

"Like hell," she heard him mutter as she descended the steps to see what her ex could possibly want.

Victoria didn't want to play the alpha male drama game so she ignored Stefan's remark. All she cared about now was why Alex had showed up here like he still had a right to.

"Victoria," he greeted her as she came to the base of the steps. "You look beautiful as always."

Crossing her arms over her chest, she thanked God that seeing him did absolutely nothing for her.

"What are you doing here, Alex?"

His eyes darted over her shoulder, then back. "Can we talk privately?"

"You're kidding, right?" Stefan asked from behind her.

Victoria turned, gave him the silent "shut up" look, and turned back to Alex. "Whatever you want to say, say it so Stefan and I can go inside."

For the first time in his life Alex looked uncomfortable. Once again his eyes darted from Stefan to Victoria, and she knew he wasn't going to say anything as long as Stefan was around. This bulldog stare down could go on all night, and she had other plans, which involved her husband getting naked and staying that way for a long time. She wasn't going to let her ex who destroyed her ruin her evening or her life.

Victoria spun back around and walked up a few steps to Stefan before whispering, "Give me five minutes. He's harmless and he won't talk if you're glaring at him like my bodyguard."

"He hurt you, Victoria. He has no right being here."

Funny how Stefan wasn't being territorial. He was upset because Alex had broken her. God, her heart melted even more. Did he have any idea how romantic, how sexy that was?

Stefan eyed her and she was positive he was going to argue, but he leaned forward, kissed her slightly and said, "He can't touch you now."

Stefan turned and walked up the steps into the house, leaving Victoria even more stunned. But she couldn't think right now about all the amazing ways Stefan was showing her love. He may not even know it yet, but he was falling for her.

It ticked her off that her ex stood behind her. She was supposed to be seducing her husband, showing him just how good they were together. Instead she was dealing with the one man who'd used her, cut her down in public and tossed her aside as if she were useless.

Shoulders back, head held high, she faced him once again and met him at the bottom of the steps. Stefan was right; Alex couldn't hurt her again. She refused to let him have an ounce of control in her life anymore. She took pride in the fact she was stronger now, thanks to Stefan.

"You have five minutes," she told him, resuming her stance and crossing her arms.

"I made a mistake." He took a step toward her, reached out to touch her shoulder, and Victoria jerked back. "Please, Tori."

"You've got to be kidding me. First of all, I'm married."

Alex shoved his hand back in his pocket. "You don't love him like you did me."

Victoria smiled. "You're absolutely right. What I feel for Stefan is completely different. I would do anything at all for him. I've never felt so appreciated and treasured as I do with him."

"Is that the money and title talking?"

Before her mind could process what she was doing she found her open palm connecting with the side of his face.

"I will not defend myself to anyone, especially you," she told him, rubbing her thumb over her stinging hand. "Now get out of my sight before I let Stefan come back out and settle this in a very old-fashioned, clichéd way."

She didn't need to tell Alex what that was. Any man would know.

He rubbed the side of his cheek. "I didn't come to argue with you. I wanted to know if your marriage was for real, and I just couldn't imagine you fell in love with someone that fast and married. I mean, you always told me you two were only friends."

"We *were* always friends. Now I realize that Stefan was the only man for me. And this marriage is more real than anything you and I ever shared."

She didn't wait for him to respond. Victoria pivoted on her heel and marched up the steps, running smack into a hard, familiar chest, instantly enveloped by a scent she'd come to associate with her husband.

Strong hands wrapped around her biceps and pulled her flush with his body.

"It's okay," Stefan whispered. "I've got you."

He walked her into the house and she realized tears were streaming down her cheeks. Had he heard everything? Fear and worry took the place of the anger she'd felt only moments ago. She didn't want him to know how she felt yet. She couldn't chance ruining their relationship.

Any and every feeling she had for Stefan totally overshadowed anything she'd ever had for Alex.

"We need complete privacy," Stefan murmured.

"Yes, Your Highness," one of the guards stationed inside the door replied.

Stefan swept Victoria up into his arms and she settled

her face against his neck. Alex's presence had awakened something in her, something she thought she'd never feel again. Love. But not love for her ex. No, she was utterly and completely in love with the man who carried her, the man who knew when to let silence express his care for her, the man who showed his tender, compassionate side at the shelter only an hour ago. The man who'd taken such joy in pleasuring her, in the bedroom and out.

Her husband. She knew she'd fallen for him, but this moment solidified the fact she was completely in love. And perhaps she'd been in love with her best friend since they met. On some level she knew that to be true. But now she knew without a doubt that she loved him wholeheartedly and without any reservations.

He'd given her the control over the end of their marriage and, to be honest, she wanted to make this relationship permanent. And not just permanent because they were friends and they got along in bed, but permanent because she knew Prince Stefan Alexander was her soul mate.

And Fate had given her the chance to see just how a marriage, a love life should be. Now she just had to show Stefan.

Eleven

He was the only man for her?

Dear God, what a bombshell. When the hell had she decided that? If she were having any notions of love…he couldn't even fathom where that would put them.

Stefan kicked the bedroom door closed, crossed the spacious room and gently laid Victoria on the chaise chair in front of the balcony doors. Sunshine streamed in through the windows, bathing their bedroom in bright rays.

"I'll get you some water," he told her, his voice rough.

"No." Victoria wiped her damp cheeks and sat up straighter. "I'm fine. Sorry for the tears. I was caught off guard."

Stefan stared down at Victoria, surprised that he was jealous over the ex, who was obviously out of her life for good, she was shedding tears over.

"I'm sorry it upset you to see him," he told her, easing

down on the edge of the chaise beside her hip. "I'll advise my staff to keep him away if he returns."

Victoria smiled. "I appreciate that, but I doubt he'll come back. He hates having his pride hurt, and my refusal to accept his lame apology and rush back into his arms really damaged his ego."

Her silky, golden blond hair lay over one shoulder, and his fingers itched to mess it up, to see it fanned out on her white, satin sheets as he made love to her again. She was always a stunning woman, but since they'd become intimate, her beauty had taken on a whole new level of sensuality.

But he couldn't pick up where they'd left off in the car, not when she was so upset and certainly not with the revelation he'd just heard.

"I wish you wouldn't cry," he told her, trying not to think about what he'd overheard. "That's one thing I cannot stand."

"My emotions are harder to hide than yours," she explained. "I can't just close them off, Stefan. I have feelings and sometimes they come out when I don't want them to."

He rubbed his hands over his thighs in an attempt to keep from reaching out to her. Treading lightly during these next few minutes was a must.

"I'm okay," she assured him, wiping her cheeks and pasting on a smile. "Really. Don't let Alex ruin our day."

Alex hadn't ruined the day, but her verbal epiphany had sure as hell put an unexpected spin on where they stood with this marriage—and its open ending once the six months were over.

He hated to bring up what was such a humiliating time in her life, but since Alex showed up, that had to be playing through her mind. What type of bastard would purposely have pictures taken with his new girlfriend, a pregnant one at that, while still engaged to another woman?

He was quite convinced Victoria's ex wasn't a man, but the lowest form of life for treating her the way he had. Stefan felt he deserved a shiny gold medal to add to the collection on his royal coat because he hadn't busted the guy in the face.

She turned her head, looking out the double glass doors that led to her balcony. As he watched her profile, he saw her eyes fill up again.

Well, hell. Now what had happened? This was precisely why he never got too involved with women. He just plain didn't understand the emotional roller coasters they seemed to always be on.

"I just had a bit of an epiphany, and it hit me harder than I expected."

A tight band formed around his chest and squeezed. Did that mean she truly felt what she'd told Alex about their marriage? Was she going to discuss it now? He sure as hell wasn't going to bring it up. Yeah, he was being a coward, but there was a first time for everything.

"Since you're so quiet, I'm assuming the mood is gone."

He nodded and sighed. No way could they become intimate right now, not with her emotions so high.

"I think we need to take a breather for today."

Hurt flashed in her eyes before her defiant chin lifted. "You've never been known for running away."

"I'm not running." He was sprinting. "You need some time to think." Some time to come to grips with her emotions that scared the living hell out of him.

Before she could guilt him more with her expressive blue eyes, he came to his feet, walked out into the hall, closed the door and leaned back against it. His chest ached, like someone was squeezing the breath from his lungs.

They'd only been married over a month. How in the world would they make it to the six-month mark with their feelings so at odds? Something about seeing her ex made Victoria realize her emotions were deeper than he'd thought. He only hoped she was just shocked by seeing Alex and once she truly thought about what she'd said, how she was feeling and where they needed to go from here, she'd see that maybe what she thought was romantic love was just a deeper level of friendship.

He rested his head against the solid wood door and closed his eyes. Sleeping together had changed things, but he'd had no idea Victoria would fall for him.

Stefan didn't have a clue about how to proceed from here, but he did know that if Victoria cared for him the way she thought she did, he was going to have one hell of a problem on his hands. And it had nothing to do with the crown or the documentary.

Love wasn't something he had ever experienced outside his family or his country. He certainly wouldn't try it out on the one person who meant the most to him. He couldn't risk losing Victoria's friendship by mucking it up with an emotion so questionable.

Love had no room in this marriage.

"So based on the information you sent us, we completely agree that this story shouldn't be kept silent."

Relief speared through Stefan at Bronson's statement. He'd called Victoria's brothers to see if they had time to meet last minute, but Bronson was the only one available. Anthony had to stay home with the kids because the baby was napping and Charlotte was out.

He'd had to leave the house. He couldn't face Victoria right now, not with her emotions so raw, so...gut wrenching. They needed a break and he needed to focus because sex and tears could cloud his vision.

He'd cut off his arm before he intentionally hurt her, but if she had feelings that deep for him, he wasn't sure how he could avoid damaging her already battered heart.

"Stefan?"

He focused back on Bronson, who had switched television shows for his sweet little girl, Bella. She was now enthralled in another program with crazy characters singing and dancing across the screen, making silly faces to get the toddler audience to laugh.

"Sorry," Stefan said. "Does Anthony feel the same way?"

"Absolutely." Bronson sat down on the leather sofa and stretched an arm across the back of the cushions. "We both believe that this story, if told the right way, would have the impact you want to make. Your father was simply the victim of bad timing, from the affair, to the public argument, to the death of your mother."

"So you'll take on this project?" Stefan asked, hopeful.

"If you trust Anthony and me to do the documentary justice, we'd be happy to. But, keep in mind we've never done this type of film before."

Stefan knew the two perfectionists wouldn't let him, or his country, down. Stefan wanted his people to see his family in the way he did, to see that his father was not a murderer, but a man who was grieving, a man who'd lost his wife after such a public scandal and had instantly gotten a less-than-stellar reputation.

With the beginning of his reign, Stefan wanted to wipe the slate clean and remove the dark stain from his family's name.

"You have no idea what this means to me," Stefan said. "I owe you."

Bronson eased forward in his seat across from Stefan and nodded. "You can pay me back by telling me why my sister called here in tears and my wife is currently on the phone with her."

Na pari i eychi. He should've known that this meeting wouldn't be simple.

"Victoria had a very emotional day." And wasn't that a vast understatement. "Whatever she wants to share with Mia, or you, is up to her."

Bronson sighed. "I probably don't need to tell you that Victoria is in this marriage deeper than you think."

Stefan swallowed the lump of guilt and fear that crept up. "No."

"And I'm the last person to give advice on how to go about keeping a woman happy, but try not to hurt her."

Could be too late for that.

"Can you at least tell me what happened today that got her upset?"

"Alex came by."

Which wasn't a lie, but it was a combination of Alex's appearance and her revelation that had her so distressed. Was she upset because she didn't want to love him? Or was she upset because she knew in her heart that he couldn't love her that way in return?

"What the hell did that bastard want?" Bronson all but roared.

Stefan shook his head. "I let Victoria talk to him alone, but she claimed he wanted to apologize. He didn't believe our marriage was real and thought she would take him back. I didn't hear what all was said, but I did see her give him an impressive slap."

Bronson chuckled. "She's only been that angry twice: once when we were kids and I tried to put her Barbie dolls' heads in the garbage disposal and once when I was being an ass to Mia. Victoria loves with her whole heart, and once it gets bruised, she's like a bear. You don't want to cross her."

Well, damn. Victoria hadn't come right out and said she loved him, but the implication was there. God, he couldn't do love, had never wanted to. So how the hell had he allowed this to happen? He'd told Tori going in that this wasn't about love, that the marriage was only about his country.

Why had she done this to herself and how had he not seen this coming?

Twelve

"Guess I had my first emotional breakdown."

Victoria sat on the simple white bench across from the guest bath where Stefan had showered after his early morning run. They hadn't spoken since her crying jag last night. He'd never come to bed and she assumed he'd slept in the spare room, but she couldn't go on with all this tension inside her body or her home.

"I guess so," he replied.

Stefan leaned against the door frame, all tanned and gloriously misty from the shower. One crisp white towel sat low on his hips, and he'd draped another around his neck. Muscles covered with beautiful tattooed artwork stared back at her, mocking her. No matter her heart's emotions, her body wanted him and instantly responded.

"I'm sorry about yesterday," she told him, bringing her eyes back up to his face. "Seeing Alex threw me off."

Stefan's dark brows drew together. "Why be sorry?"

Victoria resisted the urge to look down at the floor. Instead she tilted her chin, held his gaze and shook her head. "Because I made you uncomfortable."

The muscle in his jaw clenched, and she knew he was still uncomfortable. Was it just Alex's presence and her emotional breakdown that had made him ill at ease, or was it more? Had he heard what she'd said about their relationship?

The implications of her outburst to Alex were something Stefan was not ready for. She wasn't even sure she was ready herself, but she could no longer control her feelings toward her husband. Her heart clenched as if trying to protect itself from the inevitable hurt that would surely consume her once they discussed what her emotions meant to their marriage.

Stefan walked toward her, squatted down between her legs and took her hands in his. "I just have a lot more to deal with than I first thought. I can't take on more than protecting my country and gaining my title."

"I know, and I didn't mean to add to your worry."

His gaze traveled down and settled into the V of her silk nightgown before coming back up to meet hers. Shivers raced through her. So she hadn't completely scared him off.

But he let go of her hands, and that giant step back from intimacy spoke volumes. He was pulling away. Maybe the hurt would slither its evil way in sooner than she'd thought.

A chill crept over her.

Seduction had been on her mind when she'd dressed for bed last night, but he'd never come in, and now, catching him fresh from his shower, it seemed her efforts were moot. He was obviously having no part of her plan.

Was this how the rest of their marriage would play out? They'd dance around each other all because Stefan was afraid to confront her emotions—or his, for that matter?

She didn't believe for one second that he wasn't feeling more for her. She did believe, however, that he was going to fight that feeling for as long as she'd allow it.

"Come back to bed with me," she told him.

His eyes remained locked on hers. "I have some work to go over with Hector."

The steel wall had been erected in a matter of seconds, and he was making no attempt to let her in. But in his defense, he'd told her up front this could be nothing more and like a damn fool she'd been on board with the preposterous plan.

Stefan came to his feet, the subtle movement sending his fresh masculine scent wafting around her, enveloping her, and she knew that's as close as she'd come to being surrounded by her husband right now…and maybe for a while.

"Maybe I'll see you for lunch. I have a lot to do so don't wait on me."

And with that, he headed down the hall.

Victoria wasn't naive. She knew if Stefan could've gotten that title and crown any other way besides marriage, he would've jumped at that opportunity without question. But he couldn't get around it and he *did* need her. No, he was not the marrying type, but he was the type who thrived on loyalty, honesty and integrity…all a good base for marriage and love.

Since she couldn't actually say the words without him pulling back even more—if that were possible—all she could do was show him her love, show him they were meant to be.

With his upcoming coronation and responsibilities on his mind, he'd never complained, never even spoken of worries. He'd been right here with her, trying to help her get her line started, trying to get her to open her mind and really create some spectacular pieces.

Of course when he wasn't being loyal and helpful, he was being sexy and impossible to resist. How could she not love a man like that? And how could he not see that he loved her?

Stefan had been gone all day, but he was due to return home soon. Victoria had requested Hector remain in the front of the house and only to come around back in a dire emergency.

With a deep breath, she set her plan in motion by dipping her bare foot into the pool and gliding it along. Yeah, that would be refreshing once she submerged her entire body…nude.

Okay, so maybe there was a little bit of a reckless side to her, but Stefan brought it out. No way would she ever have thought to get into her infinity pool overlooking the L.A. skyline while wearing nothing but a suntan and a hair clip.

And no way in hell would she ever have done something like this for Alex.

Looking back she could admit that she'd been in love with Stefan for years, but it took the intimacy, the devotion, to finally open her eyes to her true Prince Charming. But she'd never really thought of him as a prince. To her he was her best friend, her confidant, now her lover and husband.

This afternoon they'd ended up sharing a strained lunch and he'd informed her he'd be busy the rest of the day—but at least he'd come for lunch. He had gone into her spare office to check emails and talk with Hector about the coronation. She let him do his thing because that whole royalty territory wasn't her forte. But she was going to have to get more comfortable with it because she intended to stick out this marriage, title and all. And while she was afraid of what being a queen truly meant, she wasn't afraid to sacrifice herself for the man she loved.

While she'd never played the meek and mild woman before, doing so with the title of queen wasn't even an option. She loved being able to assist with charities and use her name and title to help others. And when Stefan had taken charge with the Veterans' Homeless Shelter, her heart had melted. That's the type of work she wanted to get behind. That's the part of being royalty she could completely embrace.

Victoria slid out of her short silk robe and let it puddle next to the steps. The thick candles she'd lit all around the pool added just that extra bit of romance. When Stefan stepped out onto her patio, she wanted him to take in the scene: discarded red silk robe, flickering candlelight and his wife naked in the water.

She may be uncomfortable with this, but she was a Dane and everything was about setting the stage to pack a punch with the audience. And there was only one audience member she cared about.

Now all she had to do was float lazily on her back, wait and fantasize about how spectacular this night would be. Hopefully Stefan would see the way she stepped outside her comfort zone for him, and if he did, surely he'd realize that her love knew no limits.

And perhaps he could step out of his comfort zone, too.

Stefan raked his hands through his hair. His coronation was scheduled to take place in a few months and he was trying to get a start for this documentary so he could at least assure his people that a new era was going to begin, starting with the truth, to remove the black mark hovering over his father's name.

His investigators had found several people who were

willing to speak on camera if a film was produced. Hector had been working behind the scenes, as well, jotting down key things he remembered from that time...after all, the man had also been the assistant to Stefan's father and knew more than most.

But right now his mind was still plagued by the awkwardness with Victoria. He knew she'd picked up on the distance he'd put between them, but he needed the time to process everything. And he still hadn't come to a damn conclusion.

He made his way up to their room, where he fully expected her to be, so he was surprised to see a note resting on her pillow.

Meet me at the pool.

Intrigued, he tossed the note aside and headed back downstairs. When he stepped through the double glass doors, he stopped, taking in the ambiance all at once.

"I'm dreaming. No way is the prim and proper Victoria Dane skinny-dipping out in the open."

She moved through the darkened water like she had all the confidence in the world. "You've been trying since we met to get me here. I thought I'd put you out of your misery."

Arousal shot through him even harder as she flipped, floating on her back with those breasts poking out of the water. His palms itched to touch them. He'd been without her for two days. Way too damn long.

He pulled his T-shirt over his head and tossed it aside. After toeing off his shoes, he unfastened his pants and slid his boxer briefs down, then kicked them aside, as well. There was only so much willpower a man could have.

For a moment he simply stared. Finding a naked woman in a pool was every man's fantasy, but he wasn't stupid.

He knew how her mind worked. She was trying to draw him back into her web and she was spinning it beautifully.

"Are you going to stand there all night?" she asked. "I'm pretty lonely in here."

Like he needed another invitation.

Stefan didn't even bother with the steps. He dove right in, making sure he reached his hands out toward her body. As he came up, he glided his palms over every wet, luscious curve.

"You feel amazing," he muttered when his face was next to hers. "It takes a lot to surprise me, Tori. I honestly never dreamed you would've given into this skinny-dipping thing."

A naughty smile spread across her lips. "Well, when you first asked me, you just wanted to see me naked. Then it just became a game to see if I'd cave. But you've been working so hard, I thought you deserved a reward."

He nipped her chin, her jaw, all the while keeping his arms wrapped around her waist. "Reward, huh? I think I'll reward you for making a part of my fantasy come true."

Her gaze locked on his as her brows drew together. "A part? What am I missing?"

"I wanted you in the palace pool. On my turf."

Victoria rolled her eyes. "No way. Do you know how many staff members you have? There's never a moment of privacy there. At least here I only had to tell Hector to stay out front since the other guard is off for the night."

Stefan smiled. "I'm not complaining."

Resting a delicate hand on his bare chest, Victoria smiled. "I just want to enjoy our time together. However long it may be."

Something flipped in Stefan's heart—something he didn't want to explore or identify.

His arms tightened around her waist. Her vibrant blue

eyes, sparkling from the candlelight and full moon, studied his face. She bit her bottom lip as her gaze darted down.

"What is it?" he asked, tipping her chin up so she would look at him again.

"What will happen after the coronation?"

A sliver of fear slid through him. Was she thinking of staying at the end of the six months? Surprisingly, he wanted her to, but he didn't want her love...not in the way he feared she was heading.

Damn it. He was a selfish bastard. He couldn't have it both ways. He either had to let her go after the coronation or step up and face her feelings. He wasn't crazy about either of his options.

How could he love someone forever? He'd never thought that far ahead when it came to a relationship. Living in the moment was more his speed. What if he tried loving her and a year into the "real" marriage he decided he wasn't cut out for it? She'd be even more hurt. And Victoria deserved better than that.

Why did he have to choose? Hadn't he laid out a fool-proof, simple plan before they married?

"I don't want to put a damper on this party," she told him. "Forget I asked. Just tell me what you want right now."

Everything she was willing to give.

She deserves better than what you're willing to give. She's sacrificed everything for you. Her heart is yours if you'll take it. If not, she'll get tired and leave, you selfish jerk.

Her wet body molded against his and her hips rocked against him as her arms encircled his neck. He wasn't going to explore further than right now. He didn't want to keep seeing that hurt seep into her eyes.

For now he would be a self-centered bastard and take

what she offered. In the end, when she realized she couldn't change him and needed more, she would walk away. And he would get what he deserved. But until that day, he'd enjoy every moment of being married to his best friend.

Victoria was just too damn sexy and tempting to turn away. And he knew by taking what she was offering, he was damning their friendship because he had a feeling she'd be leaving soon.

Thirteen

The shrill ringing of the phone jarred Victoria from an amazing dream. The second ring had her slapping a hand over the cell that sat next to her bed only to realize the ring wasn't coming from her cell, but from Stefan's.

If this was another woman…

Surely not. Those calls seemed to have either died down, or Stefan was doing a good job of intervening before she knew.

She glanced over, noting the man was completely out—if his heavy breathing meant anything. And he claimed *she* snored? Reaching across him, she grabbed his cell and answered it.

"Hello?"

"Victoria?"

"Yes." Not recognizing the woman's voice, she moved away from the bed and toward the balcony doors. "Who is this?"

The lady on the other end sniffed. Was she crying?

"This…this is Karina. Mikos's wife. He's been in a rock-climbing accident." Karina wept, and static came through the phone before she continued. "I need Stefan to come home."

Panic gripping her, Victoria looked back to her husband, knowing when she woke him she'd have to tell him news that could possibly change his life forever. This could not be happening.

"Of course," Victoria agreed. "We'll be there as soon as we can."

"Please hurry. The doctors aren't hopeful," Karina cried. "His injuries are substantial. He's in surgery now."

A sickening pit in her stomach threatened to rise in her throat. What would Stefan do if he lost his brother? He'd just lost his father. Fate couldn't be this cruel. Besides, Stefan and his brother were expert rock climbers. What could've gone wrong?

"As soon as my pilot is ready we'll be on the plane," she assured Karina. "Please keep us updated and try to be strong."

Her sister-in-law said a watery thank-you and hung up. Victoria stepped onto the balcony to call her pilot. Even at five o'clock in the morning, he wouldn't mind. He'd been a loyal employee to her family for years, and last-minute things occasionally arose.

Once she had the pilot readying the plane, she took a deep breath and bolstered up her courage to wake Stefan and tell him the news. She needed to stay strong and positive and be there for him no matter what.

When she sank down on the edge of his side of the bed, he roused and his lids fluttered. He flashed that sweet smile she'd grown to love waking up to, and she tried to return the gesture, but her eyes filled with tears.

So much for being strong.

"What happened? I thought I heard the phone ring." He glanced at the clock on the nightstand then back to her as if realizing early morning calls were almost never good news. "Victoria?"

"Your brother was in an accident. We need to get back home."

Stefan jerked up in bed. "What kind of accident? Who called?"

"Karina called and Mikos is in surgery. He was in a rock-climbing accident. That's all I know."

Stefan closed his eyes, shaking his head. "I need to call your pilot."

She laid a hand on his arm, waiting for him to open his eyes and look at her. "Already done. Now get dressed and let's go."

"Wait." He grabbed her hand as she started to rise from the bed. "You don't need to go."

Hurt threatened to seep in. "You don't want me to?"

"Yes, I want you to, but you're so busy here designing your bridal collection, and your brothers may need you on the set."

She'd drop everything without even thinking for the man she loved. Didn't he realize that?

"Do you think I'd choose any of that over family?" she asked.

He studied her face, then nodded. "No, I know what's most important to you." He lifted her hand to his lips and kissed her knuckles. "Thank you for making my family yours."

"We're a team, Stefan." She came to her feet. "Now let's get changed and I'll throw some things into a suitcase."

They worked in a rushed silence to get out the door and to the airport. By the time they boarded the plane, along with the guards, she could tell Stefan was a ball of nerves. He hadn't spoken, hadn't even really glanced her way. He was lost in thought and she had no doubt he was not only feeling helpless, he was reminded of the fact that his mother was gone and his father had just passed away eight months ago.

"It will be okay," she assured him, placing her hand over his during the takeoff. "Once we arrive and you can see him, you'll feel better."

Stefan merely nodded and Victoria knew he wasn't in a chatty, lift-your-spirits type of mood, but she wanted to stay positive for him and wanted him to know she was there.

"I know you're trying to help," he told her, squeezing her hand. "But you being here is really all I need right now."

Victoria swallowed her fear. "I wouldn't be anywhere else."

Stefan held on to Victoria's hand as they made their way down the hospital corridor. The gleaming white floors and antiseptic smell did nothing to ease his mind. He wanted to see his brother. Wanted to see that he was going to be okay and know what the hell had happened. He and Mikos had practically been raised climbing those rocks in Kalymnos. They climbed the hardest, most dangerous rocks for fun, and people had always tried to warn them they were risking too much.

He couldn't lose his last family member. He refused to believe fate would be that cruel to him.

As he approached the nurses' desk to ask where his brother's room was, Karina came rushing toward him, throwing her arms around his waist and holding tight.

"Oh, thank God you're here," she sobbed into his chest

before lifting her tear-stained face to look up at him. "He's out of surgery and so far he's holding his own."

Stefan held on to his sister-in-law's slender shoulders. "What's the prognosis?"

"Better than when he first arrived," she told him, tears pooling in her red-rimmed eyes. "They didn't think he'd make it through surgery. But since he has, they are monitoring him. He has…"

She dropped her head to her chest, sobbing once again. Stefan pulled her close, and as much as he wanted to know what the hell they were up against, he also knew the most important thing—his brother was alive. Karina had been here for hours all alone, and right now she needed someone to comfort her.

"I'll go see what the doctor says," Victoria whispered behind him.

He nodded and led Karina over to the sofa. "Would you like some water?"

Easing back from him, she shook her head and toyed with the tissue she had clutched in her hand. "No."

"Have you eaten?"

Again she shook her head.

"Victoria would be happy to get you something, or you can go and we will stay here," he offered.

"I can't leave," she told him. "I can't even think of eating. I just want someone to tell me for certain that Mikos will be fine. That he'll be able to walk again, talk again and not be a vegetable."

That meant his brother obviously had a brain trauma.

Stefan took her hands in his. "Does he have swelling in his brain?"

Karina nodded. "They drilled holes to alleviate some of the pressure, but all we can do is wait. They put him in a drug-induced coma."

Stefan closed his eyes. How many times had they been rock climbing in Kalymnos? Countless. It's what they did. Anything to be reckless and adventurous.

"He'll be fine," Stefan said, squeezing her hands. "He's tough, and there's no way he won't fight to come back to you."

Karina sniffed. "I'm pregnant."

Stefan sat up straight in his seat. "Excuse me?"

"I just confirmed with the doctor while Mikos was out climbing. I was going to tell him when he got home. What if…"

Again she collapsed against him and sobbed.

Dear Lord, a baby? Stefan couldn't imagine his brother not pulling through, but even if he did, what would they all be faced with?

His baby brother was just as strong and determined as he was. So there was no way, even if he woke up and couldn't walk, that his brother wouldn't move heaven and earth to get back on his feet…especially with a baby on the way.

Victoria rounded the corner and took a seat across from them. "The nurse said the doctor would be out shortly to talk to us. He's actually in Mikos's room right now evaluating him again."

"Thank you," Stefan told her.

"Can I get you guys anything?" she offered. "I saw a lounge down the hall. Coffee, water?"

Both he and Karina declined and Victoria nodded as she eased back in her seat. In no time the doctor came down the hall.

Stefan stood and extended his hand. "I'm Stefan Alexander. How's my brother?"

The doctor shook his hand. "I know who you are, Prince Alexander. I'm happy to tell you that your brother made it through the surgery better than any of my colleagues or I thought he would. We will be keeping a close watch on him, but even in his drug-induced coma, he's responding to us being in the room."

Hearing such positive news had Stefan expelling a breath he'd been holding for quite some time.

"So where do we go from here?" he asked.

"Well, I think it's good that you're all here. He needs strength and support from his loved ones to encourage him. I can let you visit, but only one at a time and not for very long."

Stefan nodded. "I understand. When do you believe he'll wake up?"

"That really depends on the swelling, when we will back off the meds, and how his vitals are when we try to bring him back from the coma. This could be a long process, but right now all we can do is pray and hope he'll fight the rest of the way."

Stefan had no doubt his brother would do just that. "Thank you, Doctor."

"Go see him," Stefan urged Karina. "Tell him your news and give him something to fight for."

Karina smiled. "You think I should tell him before he wakes up?"

"Absolutely." He leaned in, kissed her damp cheek. "Go on. We'll be here."

She all but ran down the hall, and Stefan sank to the sofa. Scared, helpless, yet optimistic, he really had no idea how to feel or what to do next. He just wanted his vibrant brother to be up on his feet and celebrating the good news of the baby.

"She's pregnant, isn't she?" Victoria asked, sitting beside him.

"Yes."

"Bless her heart. I can't imagine how scared she must be." She rested her delicate hand, the one that held his diamond ring and wedding band, on his leg. "What can I do for you?"

Stefan wrapped an arm around her, pulling her against his side. "Be here. Don't leave me."

She tilted her head to look up into his eyes. "Stefan, even if we weren't married I would've dropped everything to be with you."

And he knew in his heart she meant that. Which made her invaluable and precious. He'd always known she was the best thing in his life, but now he knew he couldn't get through another trying time without her. Yet if he couldn't commit to loving her the way she deserved, what did that possibly mean for their future?

Fourteen

"Can you tell us about your brother, Prince Stefan?"

"Is he going to pull through?"

"Was this an accident or a suicide attempt?"

That last question from the slam of paparazzi stopped Stefan cold outside the hospital as he and Victoria were trying to make their way to his car waiting at the curb.

"Excuse me!" Victoria shouted with her hands up. "But my brother-in-law is in there fighting for his life. We request that you respect our family's privacy. There will be a formal announcement on his prognosis later, but for now you can put on record that this was in no way a suicide attempt. We would appreciate if you would get facts straight before going to print."

Victoria looped her arm through his as she led the way, plowing past the flashbulbs and reporters screaming questions. Thank God she was experienced in handling the media circus. Being one of the famous Hollywood Danes, she was no stranger to the chaos.

She held tight to his arm as she pushed through the crowd and slid into the awaiting car. Before another question could be shouted their way, his driver slammed the door to the busybodies.

"They've never known the meaning of the word privacy," Victoria muttered. "I'm sorry."

"You're apologizing after that?" he asked, turning to look at her. "I can't thank you enough for handling that mess."

"That suicide comment was uncalled for."

He shifted, staring straight ahead. "Yes, it was. But you handled it beautifully."

"I hope it was okay that I mentioned a formal announcement later. I just assumed…"

Stefan glanced over to her as she closed her eyes and rested her head against the back of the seat. She was exhausted. Only yesterday she'd put in nearly twelve hours designing, then they'd made love until well after midnight and had woken up at five in the morning to fly to Greece. He was tired, but she was exhausted. He'd had his adrenaline to keep him pumping forward, but he had no clue what she was running on.

"That was fine. The media will spin a story or make up one if the truth isn't juicy enough. Letting them know there was more to come will pacify them for a bit," Stefan told her. "Once Mikos comes to and can speak for himself, this will be easier to handle."

Eyes closed, head still back, she gave a slight nod. "Yes, it will. Just tell me how I can help."

Stefan smiled. Even when she was dragging and on her last leg, she was still putting herself out there for him and his family. She was the strongest woman he knew and perfect to be reigning as queen…if she stayed.

No, he couldn't think about that right now.

"The best thing you can do is rest," he told her, wrapping his arm around her and pulling her down to his side. "Once we get back to the palace we'll both try to get some sleep."

And then he planned on staying at the hospital until his brother showed a vast improvement. He needed to give Karina some time to eat, to sleep, but once the doctor had assured them all that Mikos wouldn't be waking or likely showing much change for the next day or so, they'd all promised to go home, rest, shower and refuel and return the following morning.

Stefan glanced at his watch. He was so confused on time. Between not getting enough sleep before arriving and the time difference, he didn't know what time he thought it should be. But his body knew it was time for sleep.

By the time they reached the palace, Victoria had a soft, steady snore going. He smiled. He'd tried telling her once when they were teens that she snored when she'd stayed for a movie and had fallen asleep. Like any young lady, she refused to believe that she could do something so rude… or normal. So he'd let the moment go, until they'd fallen asleep once while on an evening picnic. They'd stayed out late and lain beneath the stars talking when she had drifted off and started snoring. She occasionally joked that maybe she did snore, but it wasn't loud like he claimed.

And every night for the past three months, he'd been lulled to sleep by those soft purrs, as she liked to call them. She may think it was a catlike purr, but it was more like a tiger growl.

When the driver opened the door, Stefan carefully slid her into his lap and eased from the car to carry her inside.

The palace wasn't a small place and his room was at the end of the long corridor, but that didn't matter, not when he held such precious cargo.

He wasn't about to wake her to make her do the zombie walk of exhaustion up to the room. Besides, she didn't weigh much, not when he was used to pulling his own body weight up while rock climbing.

Would he ever be able to climb again? If his brother didn't make it, he honestly didn't know. But he couldn't think like that. He wasn't scared to tackle the rocks again, but he didn't want to do it alone when he'd done it for so long with his brother.

Victoria was being strong through this process; he needed to mimic her actions in order to get Karina through this tough time.

The weight of Victoria in his arms felt so…right. He didn't know how he would've gotten through this initial shock of his brother's accident without her. She may have not done much, but being by his side, refusing to leave the hospital until he did and then handling the paparazzi like that only gave further evidence that she did love him.

But did she truly love him as deeply as she thought she did? Part of him wanted that to be true, but the friend side wanted her to be mistaken. He could admit his feelings for her had deepened since their wedding, but…love? No. He couldn't—wouldn't—go that far.

For years he'd wanted to explore their friendship to see what could come of it, but he never thought love or marriage would be a step in their lives.

Maybe fate didn't want them together since the timing was always off. Or maybe fate knew just when to throw them together for maximum support and impact. Between his father's death, her scandalous breakup and now his brother's accident, he knew they needed each other now more than ever.

Not to mention the upcoming coronation. Yes, they were always there to offer support and for consoling, but that's what friends did, right? All of that did not allude to love.

Stefan entered his suite, closing the high double doors behind him, and crossed to the bed, where he laid her down.

He stood over her, looking at all that pale blond hair spread across his navy, satin sheets. She was such a beauty, such an angel to have come into his life to save him over and over again.

How could he truly ever repay her?

Love had never been on his bucket list, had never been a priority. Love was something his brother had found, Victoria's brothers had found. Love wasn't something for a man who enjoyed women as much as he did or who didn't plan on marrying and settling down.

Yet here he was married to the most precious woman in his life. And, if he were being honest with himself, he'd admit that being married to Victoria was amazing. But they'd not really been married long and they'd been jet-setting back and forth. They hadn't lived in a realistic wedded atmosphere—or as realistic as it could get with being thrown into the proverbial spotlight as royalty.

As he slid off his own shoes and stripped down to his boxers, he slid in beside her and held her against his chest.

How would he manage if she stayed? Could he give her the marriage she deserved? She'd been engaged before—she obviously believed in happily ever afters—so why had she settled knowing he couldn't offer her a bond any deeper than their friendship and sex?

There were no easy answers, and Stefan had a sickening feeling he was going to hurt her before this was over.

* * *

Victoria had been working via phone and email with her staff back in L.A. Between a few mishaps on the set of her brothers' film that her assistant had to take care of and a glitch in the Italian silk she'd ordered not arriving on time, Victoria was ready to pull her hair out.

Added to all of the work tension, she was worried for Stefan. His brother was showing remarkable progress, but Stefan was so dead set on staying at the hospital to give his sister-in-law breaks whenever she needed them. Like any loving, dedicated woman, Karina wasn't leaving Mikos's side. Victoria envied their love.

On a sigh, Victoria sent off another email to her assistant to remind her to check on the dates for the bridal expo she hoped to be ready for…if that blasted silk would arrive.

As she was looking at possible backup outlets for material, her cell rang. Grabbing it from the oversized white desk in her suite, she answered.

"Hello."

"Tori," Bronson said. "So glad I caught you."

Her stomach sank. "There's another problem with a piece of the wardrobe?"

His rich laughter resounded through the earpiece. "Not at all. Your assistant did an amazing job coming to our rescue the other day. She deserves a raise."

And she was going to give her one, for all that poor girl would probably have to take on in Victoria's absence.

"So if it's not the wardrobe, what are you calling about?" she asked.

"I've been trying to reach Stefan, but it keeps going to voice mail. Are you with him by any chance?"

"No. And he keeps his phone off while he's at the hospital."

"How's his brother doing?" Bronson asked.

Victoria sank back into her cushy chair and dug her toes into the plush white carpet. "The doctors are astonished at the progress Mikos is making only two weeks after a near-death experience."

"That's great. You guys must really feel relieved."

"Stefan is still like a mother hen," Victoria told him. "He spends his days and evenings there. I think he'll feel better once Mikos is released and a nurse is with him at home."

"I hate to bother him," Bronson said, "but when he gets a chance could you have him call me?"

Victoria drew her brows together. "Something wrong?"

"Not at all," he assured her. "I just wanted to discuss that documentary we are going to be working on."

Victoria sat up straight. "Documentary?"

"Yeah, the one on his mother's death? Anthony and I are thrilled he came to us and trusted us to take on such a project."

Stefan went to her brothers for a film? And didn't say anything to her? A sliver of betrayal and dèjà vu spread through her. Had she been used again for her family name?

"Anyway, just tell him no rush," Bronson went on, no idea of the instant turmoil flooding through her. "He can call me when he gets a chance."

Victoria hung up, laced her fingers together and settled her elbows on the desk. Her forehead rested against her hands and she refused to let her past relationship make her have doubts and fears about this one.

Stefan was not Alex. Alex had used her to gain an upper hand in Hollywood. To be part of the Danes, to be on camera whenever possible and to gain access to her famous brothers.

Alex had never loved her the way she had him—or

thought she had—he'd only been with her to see how far he could get with his goal of becoming famous.

A ball of dread filled her stomach.

Was Stefan using her? He'd technically used her to gain his title, but she knew about that and was happy to help. But was he using her as a way to get to her brothers? To make sure that he was in the family and make it that much harder for Bronson and Anthony to turn him down?

And what was this documentary about his mother's death? She had no idea he was even thinking such a thing. Oh, she'd known about the scandalous way the media had portrayed the accident, but Victoria had never believed the late King Alexander had anything to do with his wife's death. The media just wanted to make it a Princess Grace type of story and glamorize something that was so tragic.

So why hadn't he told her? And what else had he been hiding?

Had he lied about other things—like all those calls from other women? Had he not answered them because she'd been sitting right there?

Oh, God, she was going to be sick.

Before her humiliation with Alex she never would've entertained such terrible thoughts about Stefan and wouldn't be analyzing this situation so hard, but she'd been burned so badly, she was still scarred.

On a groan, she dropped her arms, headed to the desk and tried to come up with some plausible explanation for all of this. But she couldn't defend him. He'd taken her already battered heart and pressed harder on the bruise.

Victoria had to confront him, and she knew if he told her he had indeed used her, lied to her, she would not be able to stay married to a man who had humiliated her like that.

She'd thought Stefan was different. How could she have made the same mistake twice?

Fifteen

When stress overcame Victoria, she did what she knew best. She designed.

She grabbed a notepad and pencil from the drawer of Stefan's desk in the master suite and took it to the balcony overlooking the Mediterranean Sea. The tranquility, the peacefulness of the crystal-blue water ebbing and flowing to the shore should've calmed her nerves.

Unfortunately when you were lied to, even by omission, nothing could relieve the hurt and betrayal. Not even the beauty of the country she was legally the next queen over.

But the deception wouldn't have been so bad, so crippling if it hadn't come from her best friend…the one person outside her family she depended on, cared for. Loved.

Victoria dropped to a cushy white chaise and began sweeping her pencil across the paper. Soon a dress formed, but not just any dress. Her wedding dress. The dress she'd taken vows in, promising to love, honor and cherish her husband. The dress she'd designed for a princess.

Letting the pad fall to her lap, Victoria closed her eyes and leaned back against the chair. Why did life have to be so complicated, so…corrupt? Didn't anyone tell the full truth anymore? Was she naive in taking people at their word?

But she hadn't just taken anyone at their word; she'd taken Stefan at his. The rock of stability who had always been there for her. How dare he do that to her emotions, her heart? He of all people knew how she'd been battered and bruised. Why hadn't he come to her with the idea of the documentary? Why go to her brothers behind her back?

Another crippling ache spread through her, and she had no idea where to put these emotions. Did she cry, throw something, pack her bags and leave?

"There you are."

At the sound of Stefan's voice, Victoria turned her head. With a smile on his handsome face, he strode through the open patio doors. And she knew how to handle this situation. Right now she couldn't look at him as her best friend, couldn't see him as the man whom she'd confided in for years. No, she had to see him as was—a man who'd lied to her.

"Sketching another gown?" he asked, leaning down to her notepad. "That's the dress you wore for our wedding. Why are you drawing it again?"

Laying the pad aside, she came to her feet, ready to take the blow of the truth…if he revealed it.

"Just remembering the day I married my best friend," she told him, watching his eyes. "The day we promised to be faithful and honor each other. And even though I had my doubts and worries, I knew you'd never hurt me because we have something special."

He tipped his head to the side. "Everything all right, Tori?"

A sad smile spread across her face. "Not really. You see, I married you because you needed me and I wanted to get over the pain and humiliation of my last relationship. You promised to provide me with that support and stability. You promised to never hurt me, and I assumed that meant honesty, as well. Obviously I was wrong."

He reached for her, touching her arm, and she didn't step back. Because even though he'd damaged something inside, she still craved his touch. But she wasn't begging for his love. Never again would she put her heart on the line for such foolishness. And damn him for destroying that dream.

"What happened?" he asked, concern lacing his voice.

As tears threatened to clog her throat, she tamped down the pain, knowing she needed to be strong or she'd crumble at his feet and never stop crying. The inevitable emotional breakdown could and would be done in private.

"I learned the truth," she told him. "I discovered that no matter what your heart says, not even your best friend is trustworthy."

"Victoria, what the hell are you talking about?" he demanded. "I've never lied to you."

Moisture pooled in her eyes, making his face blurry. She couldn't lose it, not here, not when he'd try to console her and break her down.

"Bronson called." She stared into his eyes, wanting to see the moment he realized that she knew the truth. "He's ready to move forward with your documentary. And since you've used me for the title and your film, I guess that's my cue to exit stage left."

His eyes widened, and he took both her arms in his strong hands. "Victoria—"

"No. There's no excuse as to why you couldn't have told me. Not one. So don't even try. I'm done being hurt. I'm done being lied to. My God, if you lied about this, what else have you kept from me?"

She jerked away from his grasp, tilting her chin. "I will be leaving as soon as my jet is ready. Since your brother is doing better, you don't need me here. Actually, you shouldn't need me at all anymore. You're getting your crown in a few short months, but after the coronation I'll be divorcing you."

Sharp, piercing pain speared through her. She never imagined she'd be divorcing the one man she loved with her whole heart. Every shattered, broken piece of it.

As she moved by him, she stopped, looking into his eyes. His face was only a breath away.

"If you'd let me—"

Shaking her head, she stepped back. "I just want to hear one thing from you. Did you know you were going to ask my brothers to help you before or after we married?"

Stefan swallowed and held her gaze. "Before."

And the last of Victoria's hope died.

Head held high, shoulders back, Victoria walked inside, through their master suite where they'd made love countless times and out the door. She didn't break down until she was safely locked inside the guest bath down the hall.

Her iconic actress mother would be so proud of her departing performance.

Stefan's world was completely and utterly empty. Two days ago Victoria had gotten on her jet and left Galini Isle. Two days ago she'd stood before him, hurt swimming in her eyes, and accused him of betraying her trust, and in the next moment she was gone.

She'd known exactly how to bring him to his knees

and cause the most guilt. He hadn't been fully truthful with her and now he was being damned for it. Nothing less than he deserved.

Stefan slammed his empty glass back down on the bar in his study. Scotch wouldn't take the pain away, and to be honest, he deserved any heartbreak he had because he'd brought every bit of it on himself. He'd known she'd been lied to before. Why the hell hadn't he discussed his plans with her?

He hadn't called Bronson back. Who knew what Victoria had told her brothers when she returned home. For all Stefan knew, this project was over before it got started.

But right now he didn't give a damn about his project.

What he did care about was the fact that he'd damaged something, someone so beautiful. He didn't know if they could get past this trauma, not just for the marriage, but the friendship.

He had to get her back. He couldn't lose their friendship. Victoria was the single most important woman in his life, and living without her was incomprehensible.

Stefan gripped his glass, resting his other hand on the bar and hanging his head down between his shoulders. Hindsight was just as cruel as fate, in his opinion. He'd known he was using her, had known that he needed to in order to gain what he wanted. But fate had dangled all those opportunities in front of his face and he'd taken chances he never should've taken—the marriage, the documentary…the sex. Because all of those chances didn't just involve his life, they affected Victoria's.

He hurled the Scotch tumbler across the room, not feeling any better when the crackling of glass and shards splintering to the floor resounded in the room.

Seconds later his guard burst through the door. "Your Highness, are you all right?"

Stefan shook his head. No, he was not all right.

"Glass broke," he said. "I'll clean it."

With that, the guard backed out again, leaving Stefan alone once more. But alone wasn't good. Alone meant he had only his thoughts to keep him company, and it was those haunting thoughts that had that invisible band around his chest tightening.

Memories of Victoria washed over him—on their wedding day gliding down the aisle, swimming in the ocean, beneath him in bed, gazing up at him like he was her world.

If they were just friends, then this revelation about the movie wouldn't have hurt her so badly. He'd lost her as his wife…he refused to lose his best friend, too.

Victoria was still in her office. Her employees had left long ago, but she stood in the middle of her spacious sewing room in front of the three-way mirror trying her hardest to pin the dress without sticking herself…again. The design was finally coming along, and she wanted to get it finished tonight.

Working through a broken heart was the only way she would get past this. She had to throw all her emotions into her work because if she went home, if she had to stop and even think for a moment about her personal life, she'd crumble and may never recover.

A knot formed in her stomach. She hated regrets, and hated even more that those regrets circled around Stefan. Fury filled her, pain consumed her. But at the end of the day she only had herself to blame for falling in love with him. She should've known better. Hadn't she seen over the years how he was with women? Hadn't she witnessed first-hand how he'd discarded them when they got too close?

And Victoria had fallen into his trap, fallen for those

charms and assumed that bond they'd formed as teens would get them through anything. But even the strongest bonds could be broken with enough force.

On a sigh, she shoved a pin through the silk gathered at her waist and glanced up into the mirror. A scream caught in her throat at the sight of the man standing behind her.

"Need a hand?" Stefan asked.

She whirled around. "How did you get in here?"

"Door was unlocked."

She'd been so wrapped up in her anger, her hurt and work to check it after her last employee left.

"I've called you for days. You never answered or returned my calls."

Victoria crossed her arms over her chest, as if that could protect her from allowing any more hurt to seep in.

"I went by your house first," he told her, still remaining in the doorway as if he were afraid to come closer. Smart man. "I should've known you'd be here working."

"And as you can see, I'm busy."

She lifted the heavy skirt of her silk gown and turned back to the mirror. Reaching for another pin from the large cushion on the table beside her, she tugged at the bustline. If that didn't get pinned, she'd be spilling out, and she refused to ever let Stefan have the privilege of seeing her naked again.

"I flew all this way to talk to you, Tori. Don't shut me out."

With care, she slid the pin in, annoyed at her shaky hands. "I didn't shut you out. You did that when you chose to keep the film to yourself and use me for my brothers."

"*Na pari i eychi*, Victoria." He moved farther into the room, his eyes locking onto hers in the mirror. "You won't even listen to me? I've been up front with you about everything else other than the film, but you've already lumped me into that same jerk category as Alex and assumed the worst."

"So what if I have?" she asked him. "You took my trust and loyalty for granted. You knew going in you wanted to use my brothers for this documentary. Why not just tell me?"

Resting his hands on his denim-clad hips, he shook his head. "I knew you had enough going on in your life. This film really didn't involve you."

She was wrong. The hurt could slice deeper. She'd always heard that the people you love most could also hurt you the most. Too bad she had to experience the anguish and despair to understand the saying.

"I see." She swallowed, turning back around to face him. From up on the large pedestal where she stood, she was now eye to eye with him. "I've been your best friend, then wife and lover, but you didn't think this involved me. That pretty much says it all, doesn't it? I obviously wasn't as much a part of your life as I thought because I assumed we shared everything. My mistake and one I certainly won't make again."

"Tori, I can't change what I did, but I can't let you go, either. I need you."

"Ah, yes. The beloved crown and country," she all but mocked.

"Don't," he told her. "Don't let your anger get in the way of doing what is right."

She nearly laughed at that. *Doing what is right?* Fine, then, since she prided herself on honesty, she'd do what was right and tell him how she felt.

"I fell in love with you," she blurted out. Her eyes locked on his. "Crazy, isn't it? And I don't mean love in the way a friend loves another. I love you in the way a woman loves a man, a wife loves a husband. You don't know how I wish I could turn these emotions off."

When he remained silent, Victoria kept going, ignoring the dark circles beneath his heavy-lidded baby blues.

"I thought you loved me," she said, not caring that she was bearing her soul. This situation couldn't get any more humiliating, anyway. "I was naive enough to think that all your actions were signs that you were taking our relationship deeper, but you don't love me. If you did, I wouldn't be hurting like this right now. You only flew here because you care about yourself, not me."

Moisture filled Stefan's eyes, but Victoria refused to believe he was affected by her declaration.

"But I'm willing to give you a chance to speak for yourself. Do you love me? Is that why you're here?" she asked, searching his eyes. "Honestly?"

"As much as I ever did," he told her. "You're my best friend."

She lowered her lids over the burn, a lone tear streaking down her cheek. "Do you love me as more than a friend, Stefan?" she asked, opening her eyes.

"If I could love anyone, Tori, it would be you."

"So the answer is no."

Silence enveloped them, and she couldn't stand another minute in his sight. And since he was making no move to leave, and this was her turf, she'd have to be the one to walk away.

"You're the last man I will ever let humiliate me," she told him, damning her cracking voice. "And you're the last man I'll ever love."

He reached up and swiped away a tear with the pad of his thumb. "Can you at least work with me for the coronation?"

"I will stay married to you until then, but I cannot live

with you. This marriage will be in name only from here on out."

She stepped off the platform and started to move by him.

"But you'll you be at the coronation?" he asked.

She stopped in her tracks, her shoulders stiffened, but she did not turn around. "I would never go back on my word to a friend. I'll be there."

Countless times he'd lied. He'd lied his way through his teen years, lied when he knew the truth would only get him into trouble, but he couldn't mislead Victoria when she'd asked him if he loved her. Not even when he knew the truth would break her even more.

She'd accused him of humiliating her, which made him no better than the bastard who'd publicly destroyed her. The end result was the same. Victoria trusted and loved with her whole heart and had ended up hurt.

Stefan rested his hands against the marble rail on the edge of his master suite's balcony. Over and over during the past three months, he'd replayed his time with Victoria, looking for those moments he'd missed, trying to see exactly where he went wrong.

He knew she loved him as a friend. Friend love was something he could handle. But this deeper love he'd been afraid of coming from her was just something he couldn't grasp. He'd never loved a woman other than his mother. In his world love meant commitment and loyalty—two things he reserved for his country.

Victoria's declaration of love had speared a knife through his heart sharper and deeper than anything. Victoria Dane, the woman who'd captured his attention as a teen and quickly turned into his best friend, the woman who saved him time and time again with her selfless ways and her kind heart, and the woman who would've graciously helped him work on clearing his family's reputation, had walked out of his life. And there was no one to blame but himself.

He missed hearing her voice, missed knowing her smile would be waiting for him at the end of the day. Missed her body lying next to his. He missed everything from her friendship to their intimacy.

Every time he walked into their closet he saw her standing there in her silky lingerie trying to decide what to wear. When he lay in bed at night, his hand reached to her side as if she'd magically appear. And when he'd tried to take a stroll on the beach, he recalled the day he'd kissed her by the ocean, when he felt that something was turning in their relationship. He'd known then something was different, but he hadn't wanted to identify it.

He was going to go mad if he didn't concentrate on something else. Unfortunately, no matter what he did, all thoughts circled back to Victoria.

Stefan shoved off the rail and marched to his room. Maybe if he tried to rid their room of reminders, that would help. After all, he was still hanging on to her doodles and sketches. He yanked open the drawer on his desk and pulled out the random drawings from Victoria's late-night dress designs.

Something slid beneath his hand as he picked up the sketches. An SD card. And not just any SD card, but the one he'd taken from the intruder that day at the beach.

Obviously he felt the need to torture himself further because he found himself popping it into the computer. In actuality, he wanted to look at Victoria when she was happier, before he'd filled her life with anguish.

He rested his palms on the desk, waiting for the images to load. In no time several small pictures appeared on the screen, and Stefan sank into his office chair. He clicked on the first one, maximizing the image.

Click after click he saw the same thing over and over: Victoria smiling at him, hope and love swimming in her eyes, her hair dancing around in the ocean breeze and the sunset in the distance.

But the last image was different. The final picture was like a knife through his already damaged heart.

Victoria sat with her back to the camera, her face to the ocean as he looked at her. There was no smile on his lips, but it was the expression in his eyes. The image smacked him in the face. No man looked at a woman with such adoration, such passion, like nothing else mattered in the world, if he didn't love her. How could he not have realized that all this time, everything he'd felt, every twinge in his chest, had been love? All those times she'd smiled at him and he felt a flutter and each moment he wanted to just hold her near…damn, how could he have missed what was right in front of him?

Stefan fell against the back of his seat as the picture stared him in the face, mocking everything he'd had in his grasp and had let go.

The ache he'd felt for days intensified to a level he never knew existed. Pain consumed him, and he knew he had to take action or face a lifetime of loneliness because no woman could or would ever replace his Tori.

There was no way he would give her up without a fight. No way in hell. If he had to recruit her brothers, her mother, even God himself, Stefan had to win her back.

He would make her see that she *did* mean everything to him. She was his best friend, and he seriously didn't think he could get through life without her.

With his mind working in overtime, he started plotting how he would get his wife back.

Sixteen

Against her family's wishes and best attempts to talk her out of it, Victoria wasn't about to miss the coronation. Stefan may not have gone about their relationship the right way, but he did deserve to be king.

After all, his country was the one thing in life he actually loved. At one time she would've given anything to hear him say those words about her, too.

No matter the months that had passed, the pain was just as fresh, just as raw. Even though her bridal line had launched with great success, she couldn't enjoy the overwhelming attention and adoration her designs were getting.

Victoria smoothed a hand down the royal-blue gown she'd designed for the coronation. She'd wanted to match Stefan's bright sash that stretched from his shoulder to his hip. Though why she tried so hard was beyond her.

No, she had to be honest, at least with herself. She wanted him to shine. Wanted them to put up a united front for the public. If anyone knew about pretenses, it was her. Having come from the prestigious Dane family, she was all too aware of what could happen if the right image wasn't portrayed, and this was Stefan's final step into the role of king.

As she glanced in the mirror, she couldn't help but have a sense of déjà vu. This was the exact room she stood in six months ago when she'd married. Only this time she'd traveled alone. Her mother wasn't supportive and her brothers weren't too happy, either. Her sisters-in-law, well, they totally understood the stupid things women did for love.

And yes, after all she'd been through, she loved the man. Dammit, she couldn't help herself. Stupid female hormones. She wanted to hate him for the pain he'd caused, wanted to despise him for making her fall in love. But she only had herself to blame. How long had she known him? How many times had she seen a broken heart lying at his feet?

She smoothed her hair back and glanced from side to side to make sure her chignon was in place. A soft knock at her door had her cringing.

Showtime.

"My lady," one of the guards called through the door. "I'm ready to escort you down to the ballroom."

The ballroom would be transformed into a vibrant display of royal-blue silk draped over every stationary item. The bold color symbolized the country, and the crest would be hung from banners surrounding the room. After all, this was a celebration of the next reign.

Too bad she didn't feel like celebrating. She hadn't seen Stefan since he'd walked out of her office three months ago. She'd seen pictures of him via the internet rock climbing and surfing, always alone. All the tabloids were speculating a separation between them. Both she and Stefan had issued press releases stating they were each busy working on various projects, but they were very much still married and looking forward to the coronation ceremony.

Which wasn't a total lie. She was looking forward to it because after this day was over, she could divorce him and move on with her battered heart. But she still hadn't gotten the nerve to contact her attorney. She just couldn't. The thought of closing the door on their relationship brought on a whole new layer of pain she just wasn't ready to deal with. Because she knew there was no way in hell they could go back to being just friends.

Victoria crossed the room, her full silk skirt swishing against her legs. She opened the door with a smile on her face and looped her hand around the arm of the guard. Time to get her last duty as royalty over with.

"You look stunning, Your Highness."

She swallowed the lump of guilt over the pretense. "Thank you. I'm a bit nervous."

His soft chuckle sounded through the marble hallway. "Nothing to be nervous about. All you have to do is smile and take the crown."

The crown, the one that symbolized leadership and loyalty. And in a few short months, she'd give it up because she couldn't remain queen of this country. She couldn't stay with Stefan, no matter how she loved him or how much he claimed to care for her. Wasn't there a song about sometimes love not being enough?

Victoria descended the steps, ready to get this day over with. A day most women in her shoes would want to savor, relish, remember. Unfortunately, Victoria was too busy trying to erect a steel wall around her heart for when she saw her husband again.

* * *

Stefan stood outside the grand ballroom and watched as one of the palace guards escorted Victoria toward him. Her beauty had been in his dreams every night. That flawless elegance from her golden hair to her sweet smile to her delicate frame.

And every night he'd lain in bed alone, wishing he could have her by his side, wishing he could hear those very unladylike snores coming from the other side of the bed.

He knew he had it bad when he missed Victoria's snoring.

But it was the epiphany brought about by those images that prompted him to make the biggest decision of his life. One that was life-altering, but there was no other choice. Not if he wanted to have any type of peace and happiness. And not if he wanted to keep the woman he loved.

As she approached him, he extended his hand, eager for that first contact after being without her familiar touch for too long.

"You're the most beautiful sight I've seen in three months," he told her, bringing her hand to his lips.

Victoria bowed. "Thank you, Your Majesty."

Na pari i eychi, she was going to keep it formal and stiff. Like hell. He wasn't having any of that and in about two minutes she'd see just how serious he was about keeping things between them very, very personal.

She'd turned him down in L.A. because he'd been uncertain. Well, after three months of living without her, then finding those damning pictures from the beach and knowing he could indeed have all that was important, he was not going to end this day without getting the one thing in life he could not live without. And his revelation would no doubt shock her. Surprisingly, once he'd made the decision, he wasn't upset about it.

But for the first time in his life he was scared. A ball of nerves settled deep into his stomach. He couldn't lose her. Right now, nothing else mattered but his goal. And that was another first…this goal had absolutely nothing to do with his country.

"Are you ready?" he asked, looking into her blue eyes that never failed to captivate him.

For months he'd had a band around his chest, and seeing her in person only tightened it. The ache for her was unlike anything he'd ever known.

"Do I have a choice?" she whispered, holding his gaze.

Without a word, he wrapped her fingers around his arm and headed toward the closed set of double doors leading to the ballroom. On the other side, hundreds of very important diplomats, presidents and royalty waited to see the crowning of the next king and queen of Galini Isle.

Were they in for a surprise.

Two guards pulled open the tall, arched doors, revealing a ballroom adorned with royal silk the color of his vibrant sash and banners with the Alexander family crest suspended from the ceiling, the balcony and between the windows.

Everyone came to their feet as he and Victoria made their way down the blue satin stretched along the aisle before them, the Archbishop waiting at the end dressed in pristine white robes with a blue sash.

Even Mikos, who was still in a wheelchair but recovering nicely, waited at the end of the aisle. His brother knew exactly what was getting ready to take place. Mikos flashed a knowing smile and gave him a nod of approval.

Stefan swallowed the inkling of fear that kept trying to creep in. This was the right move to make, the only move to make. He had to take this leap and pray it paid off in the end. He wanted Victoria back and would do whatever it took.

Her fingers curled into his forearm and he knew she was nervous, angry, scared. Hopefully after today he could make her happy from here on out. He had to try, at least. What kind of man would he be if he didn't?

Once they reached the end of the aisle, the archbishop gestured for them to step up onto the stage, where two high-back thrones, centuries old, awaited them.

Stefan slid Victoria's hand from his arm and assisted her, careful not to step on the skirt of her gown. Once she was up and seated, he joined her. They faced the crowd, and Stefan knew it was go time.

He'd scaled the death defying rocks of Kalymnos, but that was nothing compared to the anxiety that slid through him, knowing his life and everything he loved was on the line. Every goal he'd ever wanted was within his reach… but he'd give it up in a flash for a lifetime with this woman.

When the archbishop opened his mouth, Stefan held up a hand, cutting the elderly man off.

"I do apologize," Stefan said. "But I have something to say before we proceed, if that's all right."

Obviously shocked, the archbishop stuttered a bit before bowing. "Of course, Your Majesty."

"What are you doing?" Victoria whispered beside him.

"Taking control of my life," he told her before coming to his feet.

Stefan glanced over the crowd, pulling up all his courage and strength. He'd need a great deal of both to get through the next several life-altering moments.

He glanced down to Mikos, who was still smiling. And Stefan knew that if Mikos could practically come back from near death, then Stefan could lay his heart on the line in front of millions of viewers.

"Sorry to interrupt the ceremony before it starts," he said to the crowd of suspicious onlookers. "But I have something important to say and this may change the outcome of today's festivities."

"Stefan," Victoria whispered from behind him. "Stop. Sit down."

Ignoring her, he moved to stand on the other side of her chair because all of this was for her benefit...not the spectators'. He looked down into her eyes and took a deep breath.

"Victoria Dane Alexander, you have been my best friend since we were teens. There's nothing I wouldn't do for you and I've come to learn there's nothing you wouldn't do for me."

Victoria bowed her head, clamping her hands tightly in her lap. He wanted to know what she was thinking, but he had to keep going, had to make her see this wasn't just about a title or a stupid movie.

"I've been using this beautiful woman," he admitted to the crowd. An audible gasp settled over the ballroom. "I needed her to keep this country in my family and become your king. She agreed to marry me, and I promised her after the coronation if she chose to end the marriage, I would step aside."

Stefan couldn't stand it anymore. He reached out, placing a hand over her shoulder and squeezed. She trembled beneath his touch.

"But I can't step aside."

Her head jerked up to meet his. Tears swam in her eyes, ready to fall down at the next blink.

"I can't step aside and let this woman out of my life," he continued. "I don't deserve her or her loyalty. I certainly don't deserve her love for the way I've treated her. But she fell in love with me."

His eyes locked on to hers. "And with no doubts of our future together, I fell in love with her."

Victoria's watery eyes searched his face and Stefan got down on one knee beside her chair. Taking her hand in his, he kissed her knuckles.

"I haven't been honest with Victoria, or all of you. This marriage was a fake, but I do love you, Victoria. And if I can't be your king, then so be it. I couldn't live with myself if I let this woman out of my life."

He took a deep breath as he continued to lay his heart on the line. "Victoria," he said, softer now because nothing else mattered except her response, "I wasn't respectful when I didn't tell you the full truth, but I swear on my life if you let me back into that loving heart of yours, I'll spend the rest of our lives making it up to you. Nothing else matters but you and us…if you'll have me."

She chewed on her bottom lip. "You don't mean this."

Stroking the back of her trembling hand, he smiled. "I've never meant anything more. I'm not sure when I fell in love with you. Maybe it was when I first met you or maybe it was when you were walking down the aisle to become my bride. Looking back, I think I've always been in love with you and I just couldn't admit it to myself. At least I didn't know the level of love I had. It's so much deeper than I ever could've imagined."

Victoria sighed, closed her eyes and let the tears fall.

"Can you say that again?" she asked, lifting her lids to meet his gaze.

Stefan searched her beautiful face. "Which part?"

"The part where you fell in love with me with no doubts of our future."

He chuckled. "I'm a fool not to have realized that I've loved you for years. All this time I wanted to get closer to you, wanted more than a friendship, but I didn't know what. Now I know that what I was searching for was love. And it was there all along."

Her head dipped to her chest as she sniffed. "I'm scared," she whispered. "What if you fall out of love?"

Tipping her chin up with his finger and thumb, he eased in for a gentle, simple kiss. "I've loved you most of my life, Tori. I just didn't have the courage to admit it to myself. There's no way I could ever fall out of love. I've been absolutely miserable without you. Nothing matters, not this title, crown or movie, if you aren't in my life. I'd give it all up for another chance."

"But if you step aside, Galini Isle will go back to Greece."

He smiled. "I found a loophole, finally. When it mattered most, I found a way out."

Her teary eyes searched his. "But how?"

"Mikos will step up if I need him to," he told her.

"I didn't think he could."

He took her hand, kissed it and smiled. "I'll explain later. Can you please put me out of my misery and tell me this marriage will be real from here on out?"

A beautiful, hopeful smile spread across her face. "I don't want you to give up your title or the documentary… though my brothers are pretty upset, but I can talk to them."

Stefan squeezed her hands. "I seriously don't care about anything but being with you. If you're in my future, I can handle whatever comes my way."

She leaned toward him and kissed his lips before whispering in his ear, "Then let's see if we can finish this coronation ceremony and we can celebrate alone wearing only our crowns."

The archbishop stepped forward. "Are the two of you certain this marriage is legitimate now?"

Victoria smiled and nodded. "I'm certain."

Stefan stared into her watery eyes. "Never been more sure of anything in my life."

"Then I approve the continuation of this coronation ceremony," the archbishop declared as the crowd began to clap and cheer.

Stefan hadn't seen Victoria for several minutes and was starting to wonder if she'd changed her mind and run out the palace doors with their last guest.

Midnight had come and gone and the coronation celebration had just calmed down. Dancing, laughing and holding Victoria in his arms nearly the entire evening had been the best moments of his life.

When she could've chosen to turn her back on him, on his title and his beloved country, she hadn't. She'd stood by his side, even when he'd hurt her.

And that gnawing ache would haunt him the rest of his life. Knowing he'd caused her even a second of grief made him ill. But the fact their love overcame his moments of idiocy proved they were meant to be.

"Your Majesty."

Stefan stopped in the corridor leading to his wing and turned to the sound of Hector's voice.

"Yes?"

His loyal assistant and guard smiled. "I'm to give you a message from your queen."

A smile spread across Stefan's face. Yes, she was his queen, his wife, the love of his life.

"And what is it?"

Hector cleared his throat. "I am to tell you, and I quote, 'Tell my king that the last part of his dream is coming true, and he'll know where to find me.'"

Stefan thought for about a half second before he

laughed. "Thank you, Hector. Please make sure the staff stays out of the east wing tonight."

With a faint redness to his wrinkled cheeks, Hector bowed. "As you wish, King Alexander."

As much as he loved hearing that title and knowing it belonged to him, he was loving even more what his sneaky wife had in store for him. He knew just where to find her.

Arousal shot through him fast and hard as his long strides ate up the hallways leading to the destination.

Through the wall of glass, he saw her—his queen wearing her jeweled crown...and nothing else. She hadn't been kidding about the celebration wearing only the crowns. He liked her style of thinking.

Stefan entered the pool area and began undoing the double-breasted buttons of his jacket.

"Queen Alexander, are you aware of the age and expense of that crown upon your head?" he asked, slipping out of the garment.

She smiled, rested her arms on the edge of the pool and peered up at him. "I have a pretty good idea, but I wanted to add a bit to this fantasy, too."

Unlike her, he left his crown sitting on the bench where she'd draped her silk gown.

"And what's your fantasy?"

"Making love while wearing my crown," she told him, a sultry grin inviting him to join her. "I added some pins, so I think we're safe from it falling off."

When he slid off the last of his clothes and turned, he waited until recognition dawned in her eyes.

"Stefan?"

Unable to stop his grin, he took a step closer. "What do you think?"

"I can't believe... When did you get it?"

He glanced down at the new ink on his chest. "A few

weeks ago. I found some of your drawings lying on the desk. I was partial to the one with the crest and our initials. Since I already had the crest, I only had to add your work."

"Come closer and let me see," she told him. "I want to get a better look."

He moved to the edge and hopped in, coming to stand directly beside her. "By all means, feel free to look all you want. Touching is allowed, too."

Her fingertip traced the design that he'd had done in her honor, imagining her face when she finally saw it.

"It's beautiful," she whispered. "I can't believe you took one of my crazy doodles and turned it into something so beautiful. Meaningful."

He grasped her bare shoulders in his hands and pulled her against him. "Everything about you is beautiful and meaningful, Tori. And I think this should be your royal wardrobe," he told her. "The tiara and nothing else."

Soft laughter spilled from her lips. "That's exactly how I want you all the time," she told him.

He nipped at her lips, tilting his hips toward hers. "I'll see about setting that into an order."

"Speaking of orders, how did you manage to find a loophole that would allow Mikos to take your place?"

Not something he wanted to talk about when he was aroused and his wife was wet and in his arms, but he did want her to know the lengths he would go to in order to keep her.

"When I told Mikos that our family would lose control of Galini Isle to Greece because I had to give up the title, he started doing some digging about the rules of divorce and taking the title for himself. Since Karina is pregnant, Mikos could act as ruler until the child became of age, and then that child would take over as ruler."

Tears shimmered in her eyes. "And you were going to step aside?"

"Without a doubt. I would've turned this country over to Satan himself to get you back." His hold tightened on her. "Mikos and I went to the head counsel and stated our case. They were more than willing to let him take the title temporarily until his baby was twenty-one if I chose to step aside."

She searched his eyes. "I didn't know I could ever love like this. Didn't know that someone could love me so unselfishly. God, Stefan, I'm so glad you fought for us."

He ran his hands up her bare, wet back then slid them down to cup her rear. "I wouldn't have let you go, Tori. I can't live without you."

As he claimed his wife, he knew there was nothing he wouldn't do for her. His life was completely perfect, and the girl with braces who'd once captured his teenage attention now held his heart until the day he died.

Epilogue

One year later...

Love surrounded her. Even with the flashbulbs going off like a strobe light outside her limo, Queen Victoria Dane Alexander knew she'd remember this monumental moment forever.

As the car pulled up to the red carpet, Victoria waited for her driver to open the door.

"Are we all ready?" she asked.

Her entire family, Bronson, Mia, Anthony, Charlotte, Olivia and Stefan, all smiled. They'd agreed to ride together to the L.A. premiere of *Legendary Icon.* So much had happened in the past few years, and they wanted to make a united front, to show they were a family first, movie moguls second.

The limo door opened; screams, cameras and the red carpet awaited them. Victoria never tired of the positive attention the media gave to her brothers and mother. They were so talented and she was thrilled to be part of this night, this movie.

The driver helped Olivia out first and the crowd grew even louder.

"She's going to shine tonight," Bronson said with a smile on his face.

Anthony nodded. "She always shines, but she's waited for this for so long. I'm glad we could give this to her."

Emotions overwhelmed Victoria. It wasn't that long ago that Bronson and Anthony were at each other's throats, but now they were family and they loved each other…all because of Olivia Dane.

Anthony and Charlotte exited the limo next, followed by Bronson and Mia. Stefan reached over and took her hand.

"Have I told you how *oraios* you look tonight?"

Victoria had learned over the past year that the Greek term meant "beautiful," but she always loved hearing it come from his lips.

"You've told me." She took a deep breath, ready to really change his life. "I have something to tell you, as well."

He glanced to the open car door. "Shouldn't we be getting out?"

Victoria shrugged. "They're all still dazzled by the rest of my family. I wanted to impress you with my own Greek I've been working on."

One dark brow rose. "Oh, really? And what is that, my love?"

She leaned in and whispered, *"Moro."*

Those dark chocolate eyes widened, dropped to her stomach and back up. "A baby?" he asked. "Tori, my God. Are you serious?"

With tears clogging her throat, she nodded. "Yes. I know we wanted to wait a bit longer, but—"

Stefan took her face in his hands and kissed her, thoroughly, deeply, passionately. Who needed lip gloss for the premiere anyway?

When he leaned back, he was still grinning like she'd never seen before. "I'm thrilled. Are you feeling okay?"

She nodded. "I haven't been sick once, and the doctor said I'm about seven weeks along and very healthy."

He kissed her again. "I love you, Victoria. I can't tell you how much."

She started easing toward the open door, toward the shouts and cameras. "After we celebrate this premiere, you can show me at home."

* * * * *

COMING NEXT MONTH from Harlequin Desire®
AVAILABLE APRIL 2, 2013

#2221 PLAYING FOR KEEPS
The Alpha Brotherhood
Catherine Mann
Malcolm Douglas uses his secret Interpol connections to protect his childhood sweetheart when her life is in danger. But their close proximity reignites flames they thought were long burned out.

#2222 NO STRANGER TO SCANDAL
Daughters of Power: The Capital
Rachel Bailey
Will a young reporter struggling to prove herself fall for the older single dad who's investigating her family's news network empire—with the intention of destroying it?

#2223 IN THE RANCHER'S ARMS
Rich, Rugged Ranchers
Kathie DeNosky
A socialite running from her father's scandals answers an ad for a mail-order bride. But when she falls for the wealthy rancher, she worries the truth will come out.

#2224 MILLIONAIRE IN A STETSON
Colorado Cattle Barons
Barbara Dunlop
The missing diary of heiress Niki Gerard's mother triggers an all-out scandal. While she figures out who she can trust, the new rancher in town stirs up passions...and harbors secrets of his own.

#2225 PROJECT: RUNAWAY HEIRESS
Project: Passion
Heidi Betts
A fashionista goes undercover to find out who's stealing her company's secrets but can't resist sleeping with the enemy when it comes to her new British billionaire boss.

#2226 CAROSELLI'S BABY CHASE
The Caroselli Inheritance
Michelle Celmer
The marketing specialist brought in to shake up Robert Caroselli's workaday world is the same woman he had a New Year's one-night stand with—and she's pregnant with his baby!

You can find more information on upcoming Harlequin® titles, free excerpts and more at www.Harlequin.com.

HDCNM0313

REQUEST YOUR FREE BOOKS!

2 FREE NOVELS PLUS 2 FREE GIFTS!

HARLEQUIN®

Desire

ALWAYS POWERFUL, PASSIONATE AND PROVOCATIVE

YES! Please send me 2 FREE Harlequin Desire® novels and my 2 FREE gifts (gifts are worth about $10). After receiving them, if I don't wish to receive any more books, I can return the shipping statement marked "cancel." If I don't cancel, I will receive 6 brand-new novels every month and be billed just $4.30 per book in the U.S. or $4.99 per book in Canada. That's a savings of at least 14% off the cover price! It's quite a bargain! Shipping and handling is just 50¢ per book in the U.S. and 75¢ per book in Canada.* I understand that accepting the 2 free books and gifts places me under no obligation to buy anything. I can always return a shipment and cancel at any time. Even if I never buy another book, the two free books and gifts are mine to keep forever.

225/326 HDN FVP7

Name _____ (PLEASE PRINT)

Address _____ Apt. #

City _____ State/Prov. _____ Zip/Postal Code

Signature (if under 18, a parent or guardian must sign)

Mail to the **Harlequin® Reader Service:**

IN U.S.A.: P.O. Box 1867, Buffalo, NY 14240-1867
IN CANADA: P.O. Box 609, Fort Erie, Ontario L2A 5X3

Want to try two free books from another line?
Call 1-800-873-8635 or visit www.ReaderService.com.

* Terms and prices subject to change without notice. Prices do not include applicable taxes. Sales tax applicable in N.Y. Canadian residents will be charged applicable taxes. Offer not valid in Quebec. This offer is limited to one order per household. Not valid for current subscribers to Harlequin Desire books. All orders subject to credit approval. Credit or debit balances in a customer's account(s) may be offset by any other outstanding balance owed by or to the customer. Please allow 4 to 6 weeks for delivery. Offer available while quantities last.

Your Privacy—The Harlequin® Reader Service is committed to protecting your privacy. Our Privacy Policy is available online at www.ReaderService.com or upon request from the Harlequin Reader Service.

We make a portion of our mailing list available to reputable third parties that offer products we believe may interest you. If you prefer that we not exchange your name with third parties, or if you wish to clarify or modify your communication preferences, please visit us at www.ReaderService.com/consumerchoice or write to us at Harlequin Reader Service Preference Service, P.O. Box 9062, Buffalo, NY 14269. Include your complete name and address.

HD13

SPECIAL EXCERPT FROM
HARLEQUIN® DESIRE

USA TODAY Bestselling Author

Catherine Mann

presents

PLAYING FOR KEEPS

Available April 2013 from Harlequin® Desire!

Midway through the junior high choir's rehearsal of "It's a Small World," Celia Patel found out just how small the world could shrink.

She dodged as half the singers—the female half—sprinted down the stands, squealing in fan-girl glee. All their preteen energy was focused on racing to where he stood.

Malcolm Douglas.

Seven-time Grammy Award winner.

Platinum-selling soft rock star.

And the man who'd broken Celia's heart when they were both sixteen years old.

Malcolm raised a stalling hand to his ominous bodyguards while keeping his eyes locked on Celia, smiling that million-watt grin. Tall and honed, he still had a hometown-boy-handsome appeal. He'd merely matured—now polished with confidence and whipcord muscle.

She wanted him gone.

For her sanity's sake, she *needed* him gone. But now that he was here, she couldn't look away.

He wore his khakis and Ferragamo loafers with the easy confidence of a man comfortable in his skin. Sleeves rolled up on his chambray shirt exposed strong, tanned forearms and musician's hands.

Best not to think about his talented, nimble hands.

His sandy-brown hair was as thick as she remembered. It was still a little long, skimming over his forehead in a way that once called to her fingers to stroke it back. And those blue eyes—heaven help her...

There was no denying, he was all man now.

What in the hell was he doing here?

Malcolm hadn't set foot in Azalea, Mississippi, since a judge crony of her father's had offered Malcolm the choice of juvie or military reform school nearly eighteen years ago. Since he'd left her behind—scared, *pregnant* and determined to salvage her life.

But they weren't sixteen anymore, and she'd put aside reckless dreams the day she'd handed her newborn daughter over to a couple who could give the precious child everything Celia and Malcolm couldn't.

She threw back her shoulders and started across the gym.

She refused to let Malcolm's appearance yank the rug out from under her blessedly routine existence. She refused to give him the power to send her pulse racing.

She refused to let Malcolm Douglas threaten the future she'd built for herself.

What is Malcolm doing back in town?

Find out in

PLAYING FOR KEEPS

Available April 2013 from Harlequin® Desire!

HARLEQUIN® *Desire*

ALWAYS POWERFUL, PASSIONATE AND PROVOCATIVE.

When fashionista Lily Zaccaro goes undercover
to find out who's stealing her company's secrets,
she can't resist sleeping with the enemy, her new
British billionaire boss, Nigel Statham.

Look for
PROJECT: RUNAWAY HEIRESS

by Heidi Betts

part of the
Project: Passion miniseries!

*Available April 2013 from Harlequin Desire
wherever books are sold.*

Project: Passion
On the runway, in the bedroom,
down the aisle—these high-flying
fashionistas mean business.

Powerful heroes…scandalous secrets…burning desires.

HD73238

ALWAYS POWERFUL, PASSIONATE AND PROVOCATIVE.

The last thing Robert Caroselli needs is
marketing hotshot Carolyn Taylor telling him
how to run the family business…and for her to
be pregnant with his child! Sure, he'll inherit
millions for becoming a proud papa….but is
becoming a loving husband part of the bargain?

Look for

CAROSELLI'S BABY CHASE

by Michelle Celmer, part of
The Caroselli Inheritance miniseries!

*Available April 2013 from Harlequin Desire
wherever books are sold!*

The Caroselli Inheritance:
Ten million dollars to produce an heir.
The clock is ticking.

Also available in the series:
CAROSELLI'S CHRISTMAS BABY
November 2012

Powerful heroes…scandalous secrets…burning desires.